Lawless Intent:

Murder in the Badlands

Lawless Intent:

Murder in the Badlands

Nita Gonzalez

URBAN
BOOKS

www.urbanbooks.net

Urban Books, LLC
300 Farmingdale Road, N.Y.-Route 109
Farmingdale, NY 11735

Lawless Intent: Murder in the Badlands

ISBN 13: 978-1-64556-272-6
ISBN 10: 1-64556-272-7

First Trade Paperback Printing December 2021
Printed in the United States of America

10 9 8 7 6 5 4 3 2 1

Distributed by Kensington Publishing Corp.
Submit Orders to:
Customer Service
400 Hahn Road
Westminster, MD 21157-4627
Phone: 1-800-733-3000
Fax: 1-800-659-2436

Lawless Intent:

Murder in the Badlands

by

Nita Gonzalez

Prologue

"This is the police! Come out with your hands up!" a black police officer shouted through a bullhorn.

Tete screamed at Black Manny, who was sleeping buck naked in bed. "Manny! Manny! Get the fuck up! The police have the place surrounded!"

Tete's words struck Black Manny like a fist, and he shot up from his sleep. "What?" he yelled as he reached for a gun on the nightstand. *Damn! I ain't going back to prison! Fuck that!* He ran to the window to peek out. He pressed his back against the wall and carefully looked around the window frame. There was an army of cops out front.

He dressed quickly and put on a bulletproof vest. He peeled the curtain back and looked out the window again. He couldn't comprehend the scene at first. Never in his life had he seen so many cops in one place. Any hope of escaping was dead. His only option was to surrender or bang it out with all those pigs. He had enough ammunition to put up a good fight.

"This is the police! Come out with your hands on top of your head!"

Black Manny looked at Tete, who was shaking and crying. At that moment, he couldn't decide whether to kick her out the front door or throw her ass out the second-floor window. "Bitch, you got two choices," he said. "Jump out the window or get thrown the fuck out of it! Pick one!"

That was all Tete needed to hear. She dove headfirst out the second-floor window, landing right in front of her row-house door. She was unconscious and broken up, but that didn't matter to the two FBI agents who dragged her out of the line of fire and slapped handcuffs on her.

The second they got Tete into an ambulance, Black Manny let loose from the same window Tete had jumped from moments ago. As soon as he finished emptying one clip, he quickly reloaded, moved away from the window, and took a position at the side window. He peeked out and saw two detectives trying to sneak around the side of the house. He opened fire, blasting one of the detectives dead in the face.

"Officer shot! Officer shot!" the other detective shouted. He bent down to tend to his partner.

"Shoot me! Y'all punk mothafuckin' pigs! I'm ready to die!"

"Come out with your hands on top of your head!"

"Fuck you! Y'all gonna have to kill me!" With two full clips remaining, he decided to end the standoff. He felt like an actor in a blockbuster movie. He had the crowd on standby. But he wasn't satisfied with his role so far. He threw the two remaining clips into his two .45s and squeezed the triggers.

Pow! Pow! Pow! Pow! Pow! Pow! Pow! Pow! Pow! Pow!

"Officer shot! Code ten! Officer shot! Code ten!"

Chapter One

Just One of Those Days

Damaris Martinez sat on the front steps of her North Philadelphia house, trying to shake off the sweaty, dirty panties she'd been wearing for the last four days and not caring who noticed. The other crackheads and dope addicts were preoccupied with their own misery. It was eight thirty in the morning, and already Franklin Street was jam-packed with people looking for their next fix. They all had the same look on their faces: desperation mixed with anticipation. They had been promised that some killer dope would soon be hitting the streets. That was the ideal condition for a dopefiend.

When Lil' Bert arrived in the middle of the block, all the crackheads and dopefiends scrambled up, forming a line as if they were preparing for a drill sergeant in the military. From the start, they were impatient, worried that Lil' Bert might run out of the product before they reached the front of the line. They were afraid to speak out, because Lil' Bert made his AK-47 visible to every naked eye. His reputation in North Philadelphia painted a portrait of a cold-blooded killer. His every move demonstrated the brutality he was willing to inflict on those who were foolish enough to challenge his authority or his position in the streets of the Badlands, where life meant little. The code of the streets reigned supreme.

Damaris glowed with excitement when the mailman pulled up in front of her house. Her dirty, stinking panties were sticking to her pussy like a vampire sucking on blood. When the middle-aged mailman with a wrinkled face handed her a stack of bills, she jumped from her steps, enraged. "Hold up! No! Hold up! I'm supposed to receive my check today! What the fuck do I need these bills for?" she screamed, extending her right arm and exposing her track marks, expecting him to hand her the welfare check.

The mailman gave her a look of disgust. "Lady, please calm down. I only deliver the mail," he said.

He was used to this kind of behavior. In his twenty years as a mail carrier, he had come across all kinds of people expecting him to work miracles for them. But today his street sense told him that Damaris was not about to let things go. She curled up her chapped lips, twisted her head from side to side, and shook uncontrollably. He knew she was jonesing for a hit. *Some people have no goddamn sense,* he thought as he stepped away from Damaris's house, enjoying the agony on her face. "Suffer 'til you die, bitch!" he mumbled as he proceeded to the next house.

He was familiar with the neighborhood and the people who lived here like cockroaches. He despised the way every one of them took life for granted. Every crackhead and dopefiend who crossed his path reminded him of his own family problems and of his past.

For thirty-five years, Frank had been a hardworking man, providing for his family and ensuring they were provided with everything they needed. He had moved them away to the Northeast, up on the Boulevard, because his old neighborhood had become infested. Drugs and murder had become an everyday thing. He was living the American dream, unlike the other African American families in North Philadelphia.

He'd made it out of the ghetto and was a real hero among his family members. That was until his world fell apart one night when he walked into his home and caught his 17-year-old daughter, Shyla, getting inducted into the raw hall of ghetto-ho fame right in his bed. Two thugs were ripping her back and front out, while a third held a crack pipe to her mouth. Frank's heart cracked like glass as he watched his baby girl move her head back and forth while she sucked on the glass pipe that was dripping with her saliva.

"Not my baby girl! Not my baby girl!" he'd cried. And then he tackled the pipe holder, got up and kicked him, and then went after stud number one.

"Pop, what are you doing?" Shyla had asked, making no attempt to cover her nude and gorgeous body that was still filled with the manhood of stud number two.

Frank went after him too, but by then the crack-pipe holder had pulled out a gun and aimed it at his head. "You try that shit again, old man, and I'll blow your dumb ass away!" Bolo said, reaching for his pants.

D-Rock, stud number two, pulled his dick out of Shyla's dripping coochie, while Jay wiped his dick dry on Frank's silk sheets. Jay pulled Shyla to the edge of the bed, bent her over the bed, and spread her legs wide. The smell of her hot coochie permeated the room.

Forced to watch his baby girl receive the fuck of her life, Frank Thomas cried out in agony and shame.

"Bolo, make that nigga open his eyes and watch his baby girl enjoy this hood nigga dick!" D-Rock said as he slid his still-erect cock deep inside Shyla.

Frank tried to close his eyes, but he felt the cold steel of Bolo's gun on his temple and forced himself to keep them open.

Shyla clenched the sheets between her teeth. She dropped her elbows onto the mattress, and her luscious breasts hung freely. Her nipples grew hard at D-Rock's touch. She forgot for an instant that her father was sitting there watching D-Rock fuck her from behind. All that mattered was the obscene pleasure coursing through her body like a fire out of control. But then she remembered and loved the idea that her father was there watching as she gave wild pleasure to D-Rock. "Fuck me hard! Fuck me good, daddy! Is that all you got, nigga? Yeah! Ohhh! Fuck me harder!"

Shyla felt the force of his cum rush inside her coochie just as her own body exploded into sweeping battering waves of release. Her coochie dripped with his cum.

When D-Rock pulled out of her, he smiled at Frank, and then smacked his face with his dick. Drops of cum landed on Frank's lips as he tried not to inhale the smell of his baby girl's coochie.

Shyla stood there shamelessly enjoying it all. She wiped herself with the silk sheets, then slid into her sweatsuit. "Bolo!" she yelled. "Don't shoot my pop! You'd better not hurt him!" She knew these niggas were cold-blooded and wouldn't think twice about capping her father in his own house.

Frank just sat there, letting his tears fall to the floor. "Why! Why! Why!" he cried.

Bolo kept the gun aimed at his temple. "You dumb nigga! Can't you see your daughter is a hot piece of ass? She's a ho!" Bolo said, smiling and knowing he was in control of the situation.

"Shut up, Bolo! Pop, these are my friends. They protect me."

"Shyla belongs to us!" D-Rock cut in. "She works for us. And she loves what we give her. Ain't that right, baby?" D-Rock pushed up close against Shyla, making sure Frank saw his hand squeezing her big, juicy tits, while he slid his hand down the back of her sweatsuit, slipping his fingers inside her chocolate booty all the way to his knuckles.

Tears rolled down Frank's face as the reality of the moment became clear.

"Pop, this is me. I'm a ho. I love to fuck. I love to smoke crack. It is what it is! Your daughter is a crackhead ho. Hate me like you hate the ones on the streets," Shyla said as she reached down and kissed her father's forehead.

Then the four of them left the room. On the way out of the door, D-Rock slid his middle finger under Frank's nose, letting him smell his daughter's shit. Then he started singing the lyrics to an R. Kelly song:

When a woman is turned out
There is nothing you could do about

Bolo, Jay, and Shyla laughed like hyenas, knowing those words would inflict more pain on her father's heart.

Once outside, Shyla decided to add more insult to her father. "Hold up, guys," she said and then ran back inside the house, where she found her father still sitting on the floor. "Pop, look at me!" she said.

Her father struggled to look at her, but couldn't. "Why, Shyla? Why?" he asked.

"Pop, don't blame them for this. It's how I get down. Remember four years ago when Uncle James was living here with us, and I told you he was molesting me? Thank him! When he fucked me the first time, I hated it. The second time, I loved it. The third time, he stuck it in my ass, and that's when I realized I was born to be a whore. So thank Uncle James when you see him at church on Sunday."

Bolo had stood there enjoying what he heard.

Now Frank realized why Shyla had always cried when Uncle James volunteered to babysit her. Now he knew

why she often came to the breakfast table walking as
though she had just given birth. He couldn't forgive
himself, and the guilt ate at his soul. How could he ever
face his daughter again? *It's my fault she turned out this
way,* he thought as he choked on his tears of guilt.

It had to be a mistake. This was the first of the month,
and Damaris's check had always arrived on time. She
caught up with the mailman on the corner of Franklin
and Indiana as he was just getting in his truck parked
in front of Papo's Beer Distributors. "Frank, would you
please look again in your bag for my check?" she asked,
praying it was there.

"Lady, I told you already! I don't have anything for you!
Nada! *Comprende?* Now get away from me! If you don't,
I'm going to dial 911 on you!" Frank knew that everyone
in North Philadelphia hated the police with a passion. He
wondered if he had made a mistake by mentioning them.

"*Cabron!* Motherfucka! *Negro susio!* You dirty black
motherfucka! You what? You'll call who? *La hara? Mi
hijo* is going to kick your ass, *culo!*" Damaris was enraged.
She knew she would have to hit the strip and turn a quick
trick for some "get high" money. She needed her check,
and she needed it now.

Frank opened the door to his mail truck just as a mob
of Damaris's friends—drug dealers, dopefiends, and
crackheads—surrounded him.

"*Bertito, ven aqui!* This *cabron* don't want to give me
my check he got in there!" Damaris said, pointing to the
mailbag on the front seat of the truck.

"I swear to you people, I don't have the lady's mail!
Please move away from the truck!" Frank knew how quick
and easy things could get out of control. His life was on
the line, and he was only weeks away from retirement.

Just as he slid into his seat in the mail truck, someone grabbed him by the shirt and pulled him to the ground. The mob closed in on him and kicked him into oblivion.

Damaris grabbed the mailbag and ran into her house.

"*Mira mi,* you fucking Negro! Don't come back here with the po-po! If you do, I'll murder you! Got that, *papi?*" Lil' Bert said as he pointed his AK-47 at Frank Thomas's head.

Everyone standing in front of Papo's Beer Distributors ran inside. No one wanted to be a witness, as the consequence could easily be death.

Frank lay beside his mail truck for forty-five minutes before an ambulance arrived. A sharp bone protruded from the side of his face, and the dried blood resembled a waffle on his face.

"What the hell happened here?" one of the paramedics asked his partner as they approached Frank Thomas's limp body lying in the gutter where so many others had met their fate. The paramedic wondered who would want to hurt this frail, little old man.

"This is the Badlands, white man!" the Hispanic paramedic replied nonchalantly as they examined Frank Thomas's body for any signs of life.

Damaris searched every piece of mail for her name. Realizing her check wasn't there, she opened every envelope and removed cash, food stamps, and checks. She stuffed everything else back into the mailbag and shoved the bag in the back of the cabinet under the kitchen sink.

Aching for a shot of dope, she gathered the checks, food stamps, money orders, and the little cash she had found, left her house, and headed for Papo's Beer Distributors. She walked inside, knowing that Papo was in the business of buying stolen property.

As Papo made his way from the back to the front counter, Damaris's eyes shone with hope. *"Que pasar?"* he asked in a nasty tone.

Damaris placed the checks, money orders, and food stamps on top of the counter for him to see. Papo escorted her into his office in the back of the beer shop. He reached for the stolen items.

"There's fifteen Gs' worth of checks and money orders here. Just give me a thousand cash, and it's all yours," Damaris said in a desperate tone, letting Papo know she was sick.

"What's wrong? Didn't get your fix today?" Papo asked.

Damaris remained silent, rolling her eyes from side to side. "Jesus, Papo, just give me the fucking money!" She could feel the inside of her stomach turning, and she felt like vomiting.

"Tell you what. I'll give you the money, but you have to throw in a super head job. And if you won't, then you can get your funky little ass out of my business," Papo said, feeling sure of himself as he threw his hands over the back of his chair and spread his legs open.

Damaris knew that if she didn't comply, the fix she so desperately needed would be put on hold. She dropped to the floor between Papo's legs and went to work on his manhood.

Papo placed his right hand on the back of her head, forcing himself deep into her mouth. When he had shot his load down the back of her throat, Damaris jumped up and extended her hand. "Give me the money, bastard!" she said, shaking. Every organ in her body ached. She felt sick, but not because of the degrading act that Papo made her perform. She was used to these acts. She made a living from them. She was sick because she hadn't had a shot of dope in six hours.

Papo threw the money on top of the desk and watched as Damaris grabbed it and bolted out of his office.

***

"Line the fuck up!" Lil' Bert shouted to all the crack-heads waiting to be served.

"Only ten- and twenty-dollar bills! No singles!" Lil' Bert's right-hand man, Ito, yelled out.

His words brought blisters to their hearts, because most of the crackheads only had singles. The crowd pro-tested to each other, but no one dared confront Lil' Bert.

Lil' Bert removed his T-shirt to display his tattooed body, which gave credibility to his reputation. Across his stomach, engraved in big, bold letters, were the words "Die Pig," and the word "Bastard" covered his entire back. His body was a testimony that this young buck had experienced more drama than the average thug in North Philly had. Beneath his tattoos were ten gunshot wounds that served as a reminder that life meant little to the next nigga trying to come up.

He hated to admit that he and his childhood friend, Bolo, were now rivals. Bolo had shot him ten times in an attempt to take over his crew. Surviving this attack made Lil' Bert even more vicious. He vowed to kill anyone who got in his path or fucked with his hustle. It was a vow he had lived up to so far.

Damaris knew that her son would have no problem selling her dope. After leaving the beer shop, she hurried back to the middle of the block where terror of Lil' Bert reigned. Standing in line, waiting for her turn to be served, she felt her insides turning, a feeling that only a tricked-out dopefiend could identify with. She hated the fact that her son treated her just like any other crackhead dopefiend.

When she reached the front of the line, Lil' Bert got angry. The sight of his mother enraged him to the point where he felt like choking whatever life she had left right out of her. "You better have some money or you're gonna pay for wasting my time," he said as he observed her reach into her pocket and pull out ten $100 bills.

"*Hijoito,* son, I got a stack. What can I get for it?" Damaris knew she was about to have her *cura* for the next couple of days.

Lil' Bert looked at his man, Ito, and ordered him to give his mother ten bundles, each containing ten bags of dope. Money was money, and it didn't matter where it came from.

Lil' Bert and Damaris had nothing in common, other than she'd given birth to him. She was just another worthless crackhead dopefiend in his book. If she got out of pocket, she would be dealt with just like any other trick out on the street. She had found this out the hard way, when one day she crept into his house and tried to rip him off for his drug stash and money.

She had known where the money and drugs were hidden, so she didn't waste time searching. She snuck directly to the closet safe. She looked behind her before entering the closet. No one was in sight. She took a deep breath and entered the closet. Behind a false wall there was a cutout filled with money. She reached in and grabbed a handful of cash and stuffed it in her pants. She thought she heard something and stopped to listen. She held her breath. When she was satisfied that it was nothing, she continued stealing the money. With all the money taken, she replaced the false wall and left. She snuck downstairs, through the house, to the back door. She was home free. She could feel her victory and see all the crack she would be able to smoke. She quietly opened the back door to see Lil' Bert standing on the top step.

Lil' Bert caught her red-handed. He immediately pistol-whipped her and busted her head open. It wasn't enough for him. He threw her down the steps and continued kicking his mother. He took his money back and spit in her face. He gave her a one-way ticket to Temple University Hospital.

Now Ito handed her the ten bundles of dope, and Damaris ran home. She wasn't about to stick around and tempt Lil' Bert to take revenge on her and steal his dope back.

She laid the dope on top of the table, pulled her shorts and dirty panties off, and placed the panties on top of the table next to the dope. She opened three bags of dope, shook the gray powder into a soda cap, and guided the flame from her lighter under the cap, moving it from side to side until she could see the dope dissolve to liquid. *Soon I'll be straight again.* Grabbing a dirty syringe, she placed the tip of the needle in the soda cap and drew the dope up through the cotton and into the syringe.

She grabbed the dirty panties from the table and wrapped them around her arm, pulling tightly. When she couldn't find a vein, she didn't waste time opening her legs and parting her pussy lips. She pushed the needle into a vein in her pussy, registered a hit, and then injected the dope into her stinking pussy vein. She drew more blood into the syringe and then injected it back into her.

Immediately, she felt the change in her body. *La cura* was taking effect. Gone was the pain she had felt for hours in her stomach, along with the nasty taste of Papo's dick in her mouth, and thoughts of the ass whipping the mailman had been blessed with. Hell, she was normal again! Nothing in this world felt better than a shot of dope. No man in the world could make her feel this way. The sensation she was feeling between her legs was one that only she could identify with. "Sex ain't got nothing on this feeling!" she said to herself as she pulled the syringe from her pussy vein, rinsed it out, and slid the orange cap over the tip of the needle.

Then she pulled her dirty panties from her arm and slipped them back on.

The medic arrived at Temple University Hospital within minutes of picking Frank Thomas's body out of the gutter on Franklin Street. Frank had already fallen into a deep coma by the time his family was notified.

Although Franklin Street had been jam-packed with people, not a single witness came forward. It was obvious by the Timberland print marks on Frank's face that someone had stomped him viciously.

A police officer sat outside his hospital room waiting to see if he would regain consciousness. Stealing mail is a federal offense, and the FBI had been called into the investigation. The officer wanted to get a statement before the FBI did. He wasn't going to let the Feds take his case if he had his way.

Shyla, Bolo, Jay, and D-Rock all arrived on Second and Ontario Streets, feeling like they had conquered the world. Shyla felt liberated. Never again would she obey her father's stupid rules. She had finally found a home, a safe haven where she felt love in the company of three thugs whose dreams of making it big in the underworld of North Philly were the same as hers.

Shyla Thomas was living out her dreams of being a street hustler and using her body to fit in with the people who lived and breathed the drug game and gangsta lifestyle.

Soon after she made Second and Ontario Streets her home, she rightfully acquired the nickname "Superhead" for the fantastic way she sucked dicks. Bolo and D-Rock used her to give free blowjobs to customers who spent more than $200 in one clip. Shyla was a ride-or-die chick, loyal only to those who showered her with attention, so they were always lacing her with the finest clothes and jewelry. Superhead was content to do whatever they wanted as long as her pockets were full. She loved being a ho.

Chapter Two

True Lies

As he paced back and forth in his private office where so many secrets had lain for years, Reverend Felipe Cruz knew he had to take action. He had to clean up the drug problem in his neighborhood, not because he cared, but because he wanted to become rich in the process. It angered him to see the younger generation reap the benefits from the misery that crack and heroin had brought to his community. *Why should I wait for a miracle, when everyone else is creating their own economy?*

Not many of the younger drug dealers knew of his past, but the older ones who had survived the tainted heroin scam that claimed ninety-two lives in Philadelphia back in 1995 knew him well. Flip Kilos, as he was known in the streets, had been the mastermind behind it. His prompt retaliation and terror made his gang one of the most feared drug organizations in the city.

A federal task force called Crack No More Crew had been created just for Felipe. The U.S. Attorney's office in Pennsylvania was obsessed with apprehending Flip Kilos's crew. All the while, Felipe had a stable of police officers, renowned preachers, lawyers, and doctors on his payroll.

Upon his arrest back in July of 1996, Felipe had become a federal informant, giving up his connections, partners, and street dealers in exchange for a shorter sentence: one year in a halfway house, and five years' probation.

The younger-generation drug dealers were not concerned with Felipe's past reputation. They didn't care about anyone who came before them. In their minds, they were kingpins everyone would know. The game had changed since 1996, and the young guns had no interest in the past.

Reverend Cruz knew this. He had studied the way the young bucks handled their business, and he peeped the gap that needed to be filled. He was going to be the one to fill that gap. He couldn't believe his luck when he started studying this new generation of gangsters. They were sloppy, and he was going to take advantage.

Felipe Cruz was getting back in the game, back in the underworld of the Badlands, but with one purpose—to win. *I pray that God Almighty will give me the strength to come out of the shadows,* he thought as he prepared to face his congregation. He wondered if he could stand up to the new brutality in the streets of Philly. He had seen plenty of good old Gs come out of retirement only to be used up and disposed of.

Reverend Felipe could hear his congregation singing and shouting as he walked through the curtains and onto the small makeshift altar that placed him in front of the congregation. He stood in the center of the altar for a few seconds scanning the crowd until he saw James and Eva Thomas in the third row. He paused before he reached for the microphone.

"I greet you all in the name of our Lord and Savior, Jesus Christ. First, I want to send our deepest condolences to the Thomas family for the great loss they have suffered." He pointed toward James and Eva Thomas as the eighty-plus faces in the congregation looked on in despair. They were afraid, and he knew they expected him to find a solution to the drugs and violence that were terrorizing and ripping their neighborhood to shreds. Sensing their fear and tension, he pulled the microphone close to him.

"*Satana,* Satan, has taken over our neighborhood and is threatening our lives, our families, our children, and our future. In the name of God, we can't lose them!"

He looked into the sad and tired eyes of those in the front row, and for a moment he felt pity for them. As he looked over the crowd of middle-aged men, ex-junkies and ex-cons, recovering alcoholics, former crackheads, and prostitutes, he wiped his brow and spoke. The reverend's voice echoed throughout the church, and the people cheered his every word. He dropped to his knees, raised his head to heaven, and began talking to God. This was his favorite trick! Once the congregation began to shake in the aisles and shout, "Hallelujah," he knew they were fired up and ready to hear more.

"Do you know that with God's help we have the power to stop these drug pushers and thugs from destroying our neighborhood?"

Again the congregation shouted in agreement.

"We are all fed up with the murder and destruction that's consuming us all. Mothers are losing their sons and daughters. Our young men are dying or going to prison. Sin is everywhere! The devil is everywhere! Even in this very church, some of the women sitting in these pews are filled with sin, fornicating with strangers and other married men! Some of you men, too! Lord, it hurts me to say that some come to church on Sunday and spend the rest of the week serving the devil. We must put a stop to all this sin! We must clean up our own backyard first!"

And the reverend knew just how to do it. He would use his loyal church members to carry out his plans. *Who the fuck do they think they're fooling?* he thought as he stood, wiped his brow again, and pulled the microphone to him.

"Drugs and violence are in our schools, our playgrounds, even in our daycare centers. They're everywhere!"

"Jesus, save us!" someone cried.

"Yes, Lord, hear our cries!" said another.

Reverend Cruz held up his hands, calling for silence. "Frank Thomas was fifty-six years old. He was a postal worker. He was a good man. He was active in this church," Reverend Cruz preached as tears streamed down his cheeks. He ran his white handkerchief across his face, wiping his crocodile tears away.

"Frank was fulfilling his duties as a working man!" He shrugged dramatically. "It was just another working day. He didn't deserve to die. The police claim he got into an argument with some thugs from down the block, and a group of drug pushers jumped in and murdered this good Christian man."

Someone shouted, "What are we gonna do, Reverend?"

Reverend Cruz looked at the man. "I want every one of you to report what you see. Talk to your district representative. Talk to your senator. Tell them we've had enough!"

He dropped to his knees, still holding the microphone. He waited for a reaction from his congregation. "We can take back our city from these thugs. It starts with us! If the police won't help, then we must do it ourselves!" He got up off his knees and raised his arms. "We can do it ourselves! Jesus will support us!"

The whole congregation felt the presence of the Holy Spirit.

The reverend stood silently, looking back and forth over the people. Then he focused on his trick, who sat in the last row waiting to please him as soon as the service was over. He looked into her eyes as his lips moved in a silent prayer. This was another one of his "drama queen" performances. Sweat and spit sprayed as he filled his congregation's hearts and minds with the Holy Spirit. *Who the fuck do they think they fooling?* he asked himself again.

They responded as they always did, by shouting, clapping, and jumping. Their shouts hit him like an orgasm.

"I know Frank is in paradise now, but we must hold his family together." Felipe couldn't care less if Frank was in paradise or hell. As far as he was concerned, they could all meet Frank wherever his dead ass was resting.

The trick in the back row gave Felipe a sign that she wasn't waiting much longer. Reverend Cruz nodded to her and walked back to the pulpit where his Bible sat.

"Everyone in this church must join me in the battle against drugs. We must stand together!" he cried. He pounded his fist on the podium, and the blows reverberated throughout the building. "This community belongs to us! Our children! We owe this and more to Frank! The change starts with us! I don't ever want anyone in here to face what the Thomas family has gone through."

He walked away from the altar and hugged Frank Thomas's wife, Eva. Then he turned again to the congregation and raised his arms. "Bless all of you! God bless all of you!" he shouted, smiling as he escorted his lost lamb from the last row into his private office.

Chapter Three

If Words Could Kill

Fat Angel clenched his fists in frustration. "It's not easy to set up Lil' Bert. Too many niggas are afraid of him," he said to Bolo, who was looking at his nickel-plated Casio watch as he waited for the phone call that could change his life.

"Bullshit! I don't care about those scumbags! Fuck 'em all! They can all die!" Bolo said, feeling his temper rise. "Plus, what have those niggas done for you, old head? You sit here worshipping them like they're gods, but they bleed like I bleed!" said Bolo, sensing the loyalty Angel had toward Lil' Bert.

Bolo's words cut through Angel like a razor. He knew his days as a street hustler were over, but to be humiliated by a young punk like Bolo was the ultimate disrespect. At that moment, he realized that hanging on to the past was futile. The respect the young bucks gave him wasn't enough.

In his prime, Angel ran a successful drug gang known as Blue Tape, which had put him and his second cousin, Flip Kilos, on top of the underworld. But then he lost it all when he ended up in Leavenworth Federal Prison with fifteen years to serve while his cousin became a "hot boy" (snitch) for the Feds in exchange for a fresh start at life.

Angel had returned to his old neighborhood only to find out that the game had changed. The babies he'd left behind when he was locked up were now ruling the streets, and they were more vicious in their business dealings than he'd ever been. Back in his day, players had respected the game. Now these young cats were completely blind to any respect. Everybody he knew was either dead or in prison. Only a few of these new players knew of his past. The younger drug dealers had been too young to know his name. Those who had heard hood stories about him, though, showed nothing but love and respect for him.

Lil' Bert and his crew had looked out for Fat Angel when he came home. Nevertheless, Fat Angel knew that they would never let him reclaim his old corner, Franklin Street. *It would be nice to be on top one more time,* he thought as he searched for a response to Bolo's words.

"Listen. Lil' Bert is one of my young bucks. So if you got a problem with him, take your ass down there and handle that. If you're scared, buy yourself a goddamned dog. 'Cause we both know that your little punk-ass crew don't stand a fucking chance against them cats," Angel said, hoping he'd demonstrated to Bolo that he was still an OG at heart.

"I see what'cha trying to do!" Bolo retorted. "You trying to scare me into not declaring war on the Suicidal Riders. I'm telling you now, I'm taking over the streets from Indiana Avenue to Franklin Street. I'm ready to eliminate all them niggas. So are you with me or not?"

Bolo was actually getting under Fat Angel's skin. He had helped create a monster, and now he was forced to deal with it. If he chose the wrong side, he could end up dead. He felt the tension between Bolo and himself rise.

Fat Angel enjoyed the treatment that Bolo and his crew gave him. He also enjoyed the way Lil' Bert made him feel like a legend. He loved being made to feel like he was still part of the game. "I'm nobody anymore, young buck!" moaned a frustrated Fat Angel as he looked out the window of his rented room. He knew it would be difficult to betray Bert but easy to have Bolo and his crew hustling for him. They wanted power, but they had no connections. The trick was to get Bolo to do his dirty work. He had to stay above it all. He needed to stay close to Lil' Bert to have him front him a few bricks. Difficult, but not impossible. *If Flip Kilos decides to return to the game, I'll be straight.* As he looked at his watch, he wondered what was taking Reverend Cruz so long.

"Talk to me, old head," Bolo said, knowing he had Angel confused. He had tampered with his emotions.

If Angel punked out now, he may as well kill himself, because Bolo had every intention of putting it out on the hood grapevine, which meant that Lil' Bert would have him killed just for entertaining the thought. If he went along with Bolo's plans, he would be trading in his legendary reputation for some street success that wasn't sure to come. Either way, Angel was determined to reclaim what he thought belonged to him—Franklin Street and the drug empire he once ruled.

Reverend Cruz was sitting in his office, sweating and breathing as if he were trying to catch his last breath of air. There was no point in worrying about things that were beyond his control.

His concentration was disrupted when his trick slid her tongue under his nut sack and across his anus. He was tempted to stop her, but the feeling was too good.

Feelings that he had buried in the back of his mind were now coming to the surface. Feelings that only a few of his closest friends knew were part of his secret life. As his trick lapped her tongue over his ass cheeks, his body transformed into the faggot bitch he really was. He couldn't let his trick know that what he really wanted was a man. She might expose him, and he couldn't afford to have that happen, at least not at this moment.

"Stop!" he said, pushing her head away from his crotch.

She smiled, knowing that the good old reverend was a real freak.

He reached into the top drawer of his desk and pulled out five $100 bills and handed them to her. "I'll see you in a few days. I have to go out of town. I'll call you when I get back," he said. He stood and escorted her to the rear door of the church, making sure none of the congregation saw her leaving.

He sat by the phone for a few minutes before he dialed the number. Surprisingly, it rang only once before someone answered.

"What can I do for you, Reverend?" Fat Angel's voice was a whisper, but it was animated and filled with happiness.

"Remember what we talked about the other day? I'm ready to move on my plans."

There was a moment of silence on the line. Angel knew they needed each other. It was now or never. "Yes. I'm with you. I don't see why not."

The reverend couldn't believe what he was hearing. "Let's discuss it tonight at my house. Eleven p.m.," he said and pressed the pause button on the miniature recorder he had attached to his phone. When the phone went dead, he removed the tape and locked it in his safe under his desk.

He sat in darkness in his office, smiling, running over the scenario in his mind. He pictured the casualties his plan would cause. His method was simple but ruthless. He would taint the drugs with poison and then flood the streets with them. This was his chance to beat all the young players at their own game.

Chapter Four

Operation Sunrise T-day

Lil' Bert and Ito ran the Suicidal Riders with the skill of good entrepreneurs. They had all the right business techniques. They ran their crew like a Fortune 500 company, with street soldiers and field agents on all levels. One thing they couldn't do, though, was escape the violence that came with the drug game.

It took Bert and Ito a year and a half to build their very large drug business. They were notorious for recruiting young bucks, 14 to 15 years old, from North Philadelphia— cheap and disposable. These poverty-stricken kids were provided the lifestyle they dreamed of, but it came with a price. Young bucks recruited into the Suicidal Riders had to prove themselves by shooting someone at random. The young girls had to serve as fuck toys to the stable members of the crew. Membership into the Suicidal Riders required a heart to kill at will.

Lil' Bert understood wanting and not having. He understood that the landscape of the Badlands held unsolved murders, rapes, and all other kinds of crime and destruction. He understood that if he did not inflict brutality, he would be considered just another plug in the hood. Why care, he thought, when most of his people were in prison or dead? He had evil in his blood, he breathed death, and his mottos were simple: kill or be killed, and get rich or die trying.

Ito smiled mischievously as he watched Bert patrol his turf. "Fess up, nigga. You waiting for Bolo and his puppets to make a move on us, aren't you?" he said.

"Oh, yeah. It's been a while since I went crazy on a nigga's ass. Plus, that nigga owes me big time," Lil' Bert said. As he rubbed his hand over his bullet scars, he remembered the fatal morning Bolo and punk-ass Jay ran up in his house, duct-taped him, and shot him ten times. "Them pussy-ass niggas hate what we do, and that hate will make 'em move out on us," he said.

Ito laughed because he knew Bert wanted to put Bolo out of his misery. But he had to keep a low profile because someone from Bolo's crew had alerted the police. As far as he was concerned, it might have been Bolo himself. When the police had crept into Bert's hospital room with a mug shot of Bolo and asked him to help them catch the shooter, Bert refused to cooperate. When the police realized that Bert was standing true to his game, the investigation into his shooting was buried in a box down at the Criminal Justice Center.

"I'ma fatten him up for the kill," Lil' Bert said. "That nigga will taste blood mixed with brain matter." He gave Ito a conspiratorial wink.

"Seriously, do you really think those nickel-and-dime niggas can fuck with us?" Ito asked.

"Not a chance in hell. But you got to remember something. Jealousy and guns can give any nigga heart," Lil' Bert replied while choking on a fat Dutch Master.

Ito and Bert had been tight since preschool. Their fierce loyalty to each other had grown as they got older, and although they were now only 22 years old, they both understood disappointment and pain.

Ito stared blankly down the block, observing the faces of the people he once respected. *Damn! This is the Badlands, the raw specimen of a barren wasteland,*

land of the grown-ass vulture, birthplace of body bags and coffins. All you have to do is venture down Franklin Street to see why this hellhole is called the Badlands.

His mind wandered back to his childhood, to the tiny two-bedroom house on Indiana Avenue, the place that had long ago been torn down. The apartment started out as a happy home, but as he got older and wiser, he realized his father was a deadbeat and his mother was nonexistent.

The harsh ring of his cell phone interrupted his daydream. He took the call, angry, not yet ready to face his reality. "State your business!"

"Yo, E, close up shop. Operation Sunrise is in full effect. Narcs are all over the place. Indi just got raided." Three Finger June, one of the field agents for the Riders, was on top of the roof on Eighth Street, watching for the police. Ito had slipped and forgotten that Tuesdays were bad for business.

The Philadelphia police were more than troubled by the recent murder rate in North Philly. Dope dealers were killing people over nickels and dimes, and innocent people were being caught in the crossfire. Police Commissioner Williams decided to form a task force to deal with the problem. T-day became famous for the way narcotics officers raided city blocks, paralyzing drug gangs for days, sometimes weeks.

Little did the police know that the Suicidal Riders had dirty cops on the payroll. Most of the top heads in the gang had police scanners in their cars. The field agents for the Riders were on top of their game. They had just saved the crew $40,000 in drugs, and for that they would receive a modest reward.

Lil' Bert was flaming over having to cut his hustle short. "Fuck T-day!" he hollered as he and Ito hopped into his chopped-up Bentley, driving away and feeling cheated out of their daily cash flow.

Once Ito reached Fifth Street, he flipped on his scanner and heard the police exchanging information on which corners they were homing in on for the next raid. "Nigga, we need to let our street soldiers hustle for us. We don't need to be out here around the clock," he said with a smirk, watching Bert from the corner of his eyes.

"Nah, muhfucka. I gotta stay on my grind." Bert smiled to himself because he knew that his main man was 100 percent right. They ran a successful drug business, and he still wanted to be on the front line when he really didn't need to. "I can't help myself. I'm addicted to the game. I love the adrenaline rush I get from standing on the block. The game needs me out here. Anyone who fucks with us will get blown out the water, fa sure!" he said, giving Ito a look that spoke terror. Then he drifted into some deep thoughts as the car sped down Fifth Street.

Ito grinned in admiration for his partner. He knew Lil' Bert was not afraid to kill, especially anyone who was stupid enough to plot against him.

Ito felt the sweat trickling down the side of his face as he parked his car in front of his apartment on Fairhill and Luzerne. "I have an idea that can put us on top of our game if we play our cards right," he confided to Lil' Bert, who was eagerly looking at him and wanting to hear more.

"What's your idea, nigga?" Bert asked.

Ito folded his arms across his chest as if he was searching for something to say. "My idea is to become the main supplier to all the nickel-and-dime hustlers out here. Right now, we selling five bricks a week. By supplying all these cats, we can push anywhere from fifteen to twenty-five bricks a week. At the same time, we lock Philly down and take our asses out the line of fire. Nothing will move without us approving it," he said.

Bert's eyes brightened, and he smiled to himself as he thought about Ito's idea. He rolled down the window and immediately gasped as he breathed in the polluted air that was traveling through the hot, muggy streets of Philly. "Dawg, we're at war with half of these cats out here. Plus, who's gonna run our shit? Franklin Street is our bread and butter. Niggas will kill to have what we have," he said nonchalantly, knowing that Ito was on to something major.

"Bro, we have what every cat out here desires: respect, power, money, drugs, and bitches. Think about it. It's a win-win situation. Them low-budget niggas would feel like kings, knowing that they be moving up from nickels and dimes to pushing bricks. These cats are fleas compared to our hustle," Ito said, tucking his burner under his shirt.

Bert smiled, hugging his AK-47 as if it were a newborn baby. Whatever enjoyment he was experiencing made Ito proud.

As the two of them walked toward Ito's apartment, Ito saw the shadow of a man in a dark sweatsuit standing on the corner of Fairhill Street. Not recognizing him, he reached under his shirt for his .380, keeping one finger on the trigger just in case he had to bust a few shots at the stranger.

Bert never noticed the man, and Ito didn't bother to alert him. He knew Bert would want to take action now and ask questions later.

Once inside his apartment, Ito looked out his window and recognized a man who was now talking to the man in the dark sweatsuit. Feeling safe, he shuffled around his immaculately clean apartment, turning on lights and his stereo.

Bert fell back into Ito's favorite chair and grabbed the TV remote. He surfed channels until he found the local news. Immediately, the fine-looking blond anchorwoman caught his attention.

"Mail carrier Frank Thomas, who was beaten on the corner of Indiana Avenue and Franklin Street yesterday, has died . . ."

Bert and Ito looked at each other in disbelief as the scene cut to a shot of Franklin Street where the beating took place. Two police cars were parked right in front of Papo's Beer Distributors. The cameras were focused on a young, smoked-out woman who was sitting in the back of the police car as the crowd looked on.

"Who da fuck is that!" Ito and Bert asked at the same time as the blond reporter with the microphone ran after a policewoman who was exiting Papo's.

"Captain, can you tell us what is taking place here?" the reporter asked with a smile, knowing that this particular police captain hated her guts because she made a business of reporting on dirty cops.

The black policewoman in her early forties, having seen these scenes before and having to answer the same question on a number of occasions, seemed bored by the question. She stared into the camera as the reporter pushed the microphone into her face: "The victim was a thirty-five-year veteran of the postal service and had been a carrier for twenty years. It appears that he was beaten and struck over the head with a blunt object. He died yesterday morning," the captain said, then walked away with the reporter matching her every step.

"Captain! Captain! Do you have any suspects?" the reporter asked as the cameras zoomed in on the woman in the police car.

The policewoman shook her head. "Nobody seems to have seen anything. You know better than I know that this is a hot spot. A lot of drug trafficking takes place in this neighborhood, on this corner." The policewoman knew that if any evidence was to be found, it would be found on the mail truck they had impounded yesterday.

"Goddammit!" Ito yelled, throwing the remote control against the wall. When it hit, the TV went off. After twenty minutes of silence, he rose from his chair and stood over Bert, who was still sitting down, looking at him as if he was the one to blame. "Nigga, we don't need dis kind of drama on us. It's bad for business," Ito said, glancing out the window while dialing a phone number on his cell phone.

Bert saw no reason to worry. In fact, he never even touched the old man.

Ito knew that somehow they would be connected to the whole incident simply because Bert's crackhead mother had been the cause of it.

Back down on Franklin Street, Damaris shit on herself when she saw the police questioning Papo. Not too many people were standing around, and those who did knew that if they talked to the police, they could easily become a name on a hit list.

Three Finger June stood among the crowd, listening to the gossiping bystanders. He studied the face of the crackhead in the police car and memorized the house number the police were walking in and out of.

The news of Frank Thomas's death quickly reached every corner in North Philly. The daily newspapers didn't get a chance to sensationalize Frank's death. Rumors spread like wildfire, and just like Ito had anticipated, fingers began to point at Lil' Bert. It would follow that Ito would also be put in the mix. Guilt by association was how the game was played in the hood. Ito was willing to go down with his man, even if he hadn't participated in the beating of the mailman. He stood around enjoying the intrigue and the fact that he was Bert's right-hand man.

Shyla sat in her Ontario Avenue crack house, naked, smoking her life away, and in her own way mourning the death of her father. Although he was an Uncle Tom "niggro," he didn't deserve to die, at least not in the manner he had. I wonder if he left me anything, she thought as a feeling of abandonment flooded over her.

Her family had long ago written her out of their lives. She now belonged to the streets, and no matter how much pain she was in or how many tears she shed, when Bolo arrived, she knew she'd better be ready to fuck and hustle. Anything less would be probable cause for a vicious ass whipping, which she wasn't prepared for, at least not today.

As she smoked the last rock, she reached for her jeans, which reeked of dirty pussy. She slid them on and slipped her filthy feet into a pair of old Nikes. Six months ago, she had been a dime piece, but now it was clear that the growing drug habit that Bolo and his crew had introduced her to was taking its toll on her.

"Enough with the crying!" she said out loud as she searched under the milk crate she had been sitting on for any crumbs of crack that may have gotten away.

Flip Kilos sat on his sofa, staring at the ceiling. His thoughts were on his past life. Pictures of him counting stacks of money flashed through his mind. He saw images of people on the streets lying in garbage-strewn alleys with needles in their arms. He smiled to himself, because he knew he had the power to destroy someone's life simply by hooking them on his drugs.

The ring of his doorbell jolted him back to reality. He turned on the miniature tape recorder and ran his hand over his balls. "Wait a minute!" he yelled.

Fat Angel smiled, not believing his luck. A few days ago, he had been flat broke with not a dollar to his name. Now here he was standing in front of his cousin's house, the man who had been responsible for bringing him down when he was on top of the drug game. *The second time around has gotta be a charm!* he thought as he waited to once again meet the man who could change his life a second time. When he heard the door unlock, he put his serious game face on.

Flip Kilos stared at Angel with a renewed energy, hoping to be awarded with the forgiveness he'd been seeking for ratting Angel out to the Feds.

Angel extended his arms and hugged his cousin. *"Familia para siempre!"* he said to Flip Kilos as they walked into his basement office.

"Perdón! Sorry, bro. I did what I had to do at the time, and I regret you got caught in the middle of it." Flip Kilos wanted to make sure that no animosity existed between them. He was testing the waters.

"I would've done the same if I were offered the deal you were offered. So don't sweat it. Let bygones be bygones. Blood is thicker than water," Fat Angel said, anxious to hear more of the specifics.

Staring at his cousin with deep hate as he studied him, Flip thought, *you punk mothafucka! You would have ratted me out if you'd had the chance? I'ma teach your broke ass a lesson! You're still the same stupid mothafucka who can't think for himself!*

"Why? Why now? We been out of the game for a long time. It's not the same," Angel said, trying to read Flip.

"First of all, you're broke from what I can see. Life ain't treating you so well. Second, we can help with the drug problem in the city, and in the process get very rich. Point blank, these young punks out here are getting rich off the foundation we laid. They show us no respect or gratitude, so why not take back what rightfully belongs to us?" Flip Kilos shook his head slowly. He hoped to avoid getting into details and only tell Angel enough to persuade him to team up with him.

"We don't have any connections," Angel said.

"Let me worry about that. I just need you to be the head man in charge." Flip got up from his chair and opened the closet door. He pulled out two bricks of cocaine, slashed one open, and poured out a pile on top of the mirror on his desk.

Angel was amazed and showed it. His mouth dropped wide open. At that moment, he knew that his cousin was dead serious about getting back into the game.

"How about that, amigo!" Flip motioned for Angel to get up from his chair and get a closer look.

Angel did as instructed, staring as if he had never seen two bricks before. He wondered if the two "birds" were real. Just as he was about to ask Flip if the coke was real, Flip pulled out a straw and pulled a heavy line into each nostril. He leaned back in the chair, and instantly a trickle of blood flowed from each nostril.

"Pure Mexican coke, this other brick here," Flip said, placing his right hand on the brick "This is pure *manteca*, pure dope. So are you in or are you out?" he asked, letting the drops of blood fall on top of his desk.

"I'm in! In fact, I already have some young punks who will move this shit for us," Angel responded, dipping his fingers into the mountain of coke to get a taste.

"One thing. Nobody should ever know about me unless I decide to show my face. I deal with you and you only," Flip said. He reached into his pocket, pulled out a wad of cash, and handed it to Angel. "Get your shit together.

If you're going to play the role, you must look the part. There's seven Gs there. Treat yourself to a shopping spree. Tomorrow night we will celebrate at Isla Verde. Bring your young crew with you, but keep them in the dark to what's happening."

Flip Kilos was back.

Chapter Five

For the Love of Money

The interrogation of homicide witnesses was taking place in the Round House, headquarters of the Philadelphia police and the homicide unit. A plump-faced detective named Alberto Ruiz was brought in to interrogate Hispanic witnesses and suspects who couldn't speak English.

"My name is Detective Ruiz, and I want to talk to you about an incident that occurred yesterday morning on Franklin Street. First, state your full name, age, and address."

"Lizzet Santiago. I'm thirty-one, and I live at 2630 North Franklin Street."

"Do you understand English well?"

"Yes. *Sí.*"

"We can conduct this interview in English or Spanish, whichever is best for you."

"English will be fine."

"If there's anything you don't understand, you can ask me in Spanish."

"*Sí,* yes, okay."

"You can stop this interview anytime you want and walk out of this room. You are not under arrest. Now tell me. Do you freely consent to this interview?"

"*Sí,* yes."

"Has anyone promised you anything or threatened you in any way?"

"No."

"So you're talking to us of your own free will."

"*Sí*, yes."

"How long have you lived at your current address?"

"All my life."

"Who lives at that location with you?"

"My mom, her boyfriend, and my two sons."

"What can you tell me about what you saw yesterday morning?"

"As I was coming out my house, I saw my friend Damaris having a panic attack and getting loud and shit with the mailman."

"Do you know why your friend was getting loud with the mailman?"

"No. All I know is that she was out of control."

"Does this Damaris have a last name?"

"I don't know it."

"How do you know Damaris?"

"She lives about ten houses from mine. Plus, we hustle sometimes together."

"What do you mean you hustle together?"

"We go out and get money together. You know, we partner up. Sometimes when I don't have enough money to cop, she lets me ride with her and we share our high together, and vice versa."

"Are you on drugs now?"

"No, I've been clean for five days now."

Detective Ruiz knew the whore was lying through her teeth. The look in her sunken yellow eyes gave her away. She couldn't answer a single question without moving her head from side to side. "Back up a second. What time was it when you were coming out of your house, and where were you going?"

"I guess it was about nine thirty or nine forty-five in the morning. I know because I was going outside to wait for the mailman myself. The first of the month, you know? Everybody waits for the mailman."

"And then what happened?"

"Damaris cornered the mailman by his truck, and then a bunch of guys started jumping on him. That's the only thing I saw. I swear to God!"

Lizzet felt pain in her stomach. She was hungry and jonesing for a hit of crack. She wondered, too, if she was signing her own death warrant by talking to the police.

Detective Ruiz sensed that she was nervous and uncomfortable, so he decided to play the good cop with her. He knew she was the best lead they had in the case. "Are you all right? Can we get you something to eat? I see you're very pregnant. How much longer before you're due to give birth?"

"Two months. I can't wait. This was never meant to be."

Detective Ruiz knew Lizzet was an all-out crackhead, but he needed to gain her trust. He couldn't care less who the goddamn baby's father was. *Another crack baby my taxes have to pay for! The thing's better off dead!* he thought as he continued with his line of questioning. "Do you know any of the people who jumped on the mailman yesterday?"

"Yes."

"Which ones do you know?'

"Papo, Julio, Pito, Bert, Damaris, Mimi, Negrito, Yari, and Tito. Those are the ones I remember, but there were lots of others standing around."

After wolfing down a large cheesesteak from Gino's and a cup of coffee, Lizzet Santiago felt better. She had been promised $300 and that her arrest record would be

expunged in exchange for information that would lead
to the arrest of those who had killed the mailman, Frank
Thomas.

Lizzet excused herself to go to the restroom. As she
turned the corner in the hall, she almost ran right into
Ito's cousin, MaryLuz, who was the processing clerk in
the homicide unit. Lizzet prayed to herself that MaryLuz
didn't notice her.

MaryLuz sat at the far end of the lunch counter in
the Spaghetti Warehouse, a small mom-and-pop cook
house on Ninth and Spring Garden. As she waited for her
meal, she took out her cell phone and quickly dialed Ito's
number.

Ito picked up on the first ring. "State your business!"

"What's crack-a-lacking, cuz?" MaryLuz said.

"Nothing. Just chilling. What you got for me, ma?" Ito
asked, trying his best to be discreet over his cell phone.

"I got your request. Everything is everything. As we
speak, the DJ is playing the same song. She might even
go platinum. Meet me at Porky Point, five thirty p.m.
We'll talk then. Don't forget my request." MaryLuz hung
up the phone. She too was very careful how she spoke
on the phone. It would take the police a million years to
figure out her coded conversation with Ito. The assholes
up in homicide were too fucking stupid to learn the street
culture. They thought they had it all figured out.

When she returned to work at the homicide unit,
MaryLuz photocopied Lizzet's entire file, fact sheet, her
statement, address, and the lead investigator's name
and cell phone number. She always came through for Ito
and his crew, always warning them when the homicide
detectives were snooping in their business. This allowed
the Suicidal Riders to stay on top of their game.

MaryLuz was a real knockout. She was light skinned, five feet five inches, 130 pounds. Her measurements were 36-26-42. She loved working for the system. Right after she'd graduated from Temple Law School, she landed a job in the DA's office. A year later, she went to work in city hall as a judge's clerk, then to the homicide unit, never forgetting where she came from.

By day, she was a city worker with a host of influential friends and a fan club of sugar daddies, judges, and cops who paid her well for some ghetto ass and head. By night, she hung with the Suicidal Riders, dope dealers, and killers she grew up with. She enjoyed the best of both worlds.

Niggas in the hood knew what her day job consisted of, but they also knew that, on the streets of Philly, MaryLuz was no joke. She was notorious for setting niggas up.

"Yo, who was dat?" Lil' Bert asked, still lying back on the sofa.

"MaryLuz," Ito responded, not wanting to reveal too much.

"What dat fine thing want? Ya know you should stop playing and plug me up with her. I'm good for it," Lil' Bert said.

Ito would never hook him up with her. Fucking a family member was out of the equation. MaryLuz had always treated Bert like a brother. But as they grew older, he tried many times to push up on her, but she always brushed him off. It was a known fact that Bert was a male whore. He would stick his dick in anything that had a hole.

"So tell me, what dat pretty *mami* want?" Bert asked again.

"She has some info for us on the snitch crackhead," Ito responded.

Bert's eyes grew wide with excitement. "The thought of slumping that snitch bitch makes my dick hard!" he said. He jumped up from the sofa like a kid in a candy store and went into the bathroom. He retrieved a cloth bag that was stashed in the cabinet below the sink. The bag contained two rolls of duct tape, two 9 mms with silencers, two black ski masks, a pair of gloves, and a cell phone. After inspecting the bag, he returned to the living room.

"What's in the bag?" Ito asked, surprised that Bert had a stash in his crib.

"Back up! You know what it is!" Lil' Bert opened the bag and pulled out two shiny nines. He placed them on top of the glass table.

Ito was furious. *How the fuck did this nigga manage to get a stash in here? And what else has he got stashed up in here?* Bert had crossed the line this time. "Nigga! What the fuck! Why you got dat shit in here?" Ito wanted answers. This could be his way out of the game. For a while now, he had been seriously thinking of walking away from the drug game, and with all the drama he and Bert had been facing lately, this could be a sign for him to walk away.

Lil' Bert smiled. "You think I would cross you, nigga? Damn! I see where we at now! What's wrong with your memory, Ito? Be easy, bro. It's just a small thing, a very necessary stash." He put his game face on and kept his eyes on Ito.

"Nah, nigga! I told you never to bring heat to the place where I rest my head. Nigga, you out of pocket!" Ito said, turning red in the face.

"Chill, B! Don't you remember when Lil' Jazz got murked down Eighth Street last month? You was the one who hid the stash in the bathroom cabinet," Lil' Bert said, his voice incredulous.

Little by little it was all coming back to Ito. He felt like a complete asshole mistrusting his partner. *Death before dishonor!* He replayed those words in his mind.

Ito and Bert had been tight since they were knee-high to a puppy. And most of the drama they'd been involved in had been brought on, in one way or another, by the fact that niggas on the streets felt Ito to be a cold-blooded pussy only to find out later that he was the devil himself. Ito was far from being a pussy, but he wasn't a body snatcher like Bert. He was willing to let a lot of beefs slide by.

Bert, on the other hand, wasn't having it. He was always flaming inside, but on the outside he always remained calm.

"My bad! I got a lot on my mind. I ain't meant to snap on you," Ito said, trying to repair some of the damage his words had caused.

"Big homie, dig this. At the end of the day, we both know how much work I put in on the streets for your funky ass. I'ma always be by your side. You my fucking dude. Never forget dat. Now put me down with the info you got from MaryLuz," Bert said.

Ito stared at his partner, regretting the way he'd acted toward him. In the back of his mind, it occurred to him that Bert wasn't beyond murking him. *I got to get out of this game soon.* He took a deep breath before he spoke again. "She put me on to the crackhead chick who's giving five-O information in the mailman case," he said, hoping to put the drama with Bert behind him.

"What'd she say?" Bert asked.

"Calm down, bro! We gotta meet her at Porky Point to get the whole nine," Ito responded, looking at his diamond-encrusted Jacob & Co. watch. They had a few hours to kill, so Ito made a few phone calls to catch up on what the streets were saying.

"Nigga, we got three hours before 5:30. What'cha say if I call Candy and her girls to entertain us for a while?" Bert asked.

"Nah, we gotta stay focused," Ito said, not wanting to lose track of time.

"Cuz, we got three hours to spare. Plus, you'll feel better afterward." Bert continued to stare at Ito.

"Yeah, a'ight. I'm down, but not here. Let's take them down to the Sunshine Inn on Cambria Street."

Ito smiled as he grabbed his crotch and squeezed. *Damn, pussy is what a nigga needs right now.*

Bert stood and walked into the bathroom, locking the door behind him. He sat on the toilet and dialed Candy's number.

"Hello, who's this?" Candy asked.

"What you mean, who dis? Who was the last nigga who stuck some Puerto Rican tongue up your fine ass? Remember now?"

Candy sat up in bed, smiling. "I'm remembering that sensation. You bent me over and tongue fucked my ass 'til I came. Before that night, I never would have let a nigga play any kind of ass games with me."

All the girls at the club knew Candy had the best shot of pussy in town—juicy and sweet. Word on the street was that she could make her pussy talk no matter the size of the dick, and her head game was special, too. Getting fucked in the ass was just another specialty she'd added to her repertoire of sex games. "Bert, what you want?" she asked, already knowing the answer. Her pussy was dripping.

"Damn, ma! I just want to kick it with you for a while," Bert said while rubbing his balls. Candy's sexy voice gave him a hard-on.

"I can't. I gotta be at the club at seven." She was fingering herself. Her naked body bucked and squirmed as her fingers pounded into her pussy.

Bert could hear the change in her voice. "What'cha mean you can't? It'll be worth your time. Tell me what'cha doing right now."

"What'cha mean what I'm doing? I'm lying in bed talking to you, if you care to know," Candy said, turning her fingers in circles inside of her.

"Are you playing with yourself?" Lil' Bert asked, pulling out his dick and stroking himself. The last time he had beaten off was when he was doing a three-month juvenile bid. Now here he was, sitting on the toilet, talking to one of the hottest strippers in North Philly, and playing with himself.

Candy held the phone to her ear, smiling and pleasuring herself. She was lost in her own horny world. After a minute, she realized Bert was still on the phone. Her entire pussy ached. *Haven't . . . haven't come that hard in a long time!* she thought as she placed the mouthpiece of the phone closer to her lips. "Sorry. I was just thinking about something." She licked her coated fingers. She loved the taste of her own pussy.

"So do I see you in half or what?" Bert asked while wiping his dick off with toilet tissue.

"Yeah, but I got to be at work by seven." Candy knew that a real fuck was way better than her fingers.

"I'll pick you up down Cambria Street. Bring Titi with you. Ito is dying to get with her," Bert said. Not waiting for a response, he shut the phone off.

Chapter Six

Shit Happens

A half hour after MaryLuz arrived at the Round House, she was stunned to see Papo being escorted by Detective Ruiz into one of the interrogation rooms. She knew Papo could only be doing one thing—snitching, helping the po-po—which meant that Bert and Ito would have more witnesses to deal with. She had to warn Ito of the new development, and she had to do it fast.

Chief Jackson was sitting at his desk when she walked into his office. "Chief, I have to go home. There's an emergency with my family."

"Oh, dear, what's wrong? Is there anything I can do to help?" The chief looked concerned.

"No, it's something only I can fix."

"Well, let me know if you need me. Make sure Carolyn takes over your duties for the day."

"Yes, sir."

She grabbed her Louis Vuitton bag and walked out of the building. Carolyn could kiss her ass. That skinny bitch couldn't handle the amount of work MaryLuz had on a daily basis. At the corner of Eighth and Race, she placed her call.

"What's popping?" Ito asked.

"Change of plans. I need to see you now! *Ahora!* DJ's playing another song!" MaryLuz said as she sucked in the smoke from a Newport cigarette. She exhaled slowly.

"I thought you said five thirty! I made plans already!" Ito said.

"Niggro, this is important! Meet me at Porky Point in fifteen minutes. Be there on time. Fuck your plans, a'ight?" MaryLuz was upset that Ito was questioning her.

"A'ight," Ito said.

She hung up the phone before Ito could ask any more questions.

She arrived at Porky Point at 3:35 p.m. She looked around, but there was no sign of Ito or Bert. She checked her voicemail on her cell phone and listened to messages from one of her sugar daddies. One message in particular caught her attention—the message from her hood rich trick.

"What's up, *mami?* I'm back in town, and I'm hoping to see you soon. Come through. Give me a call tonight."

Damn! This trick is crazy, but he's got money to spend on good pussy. He pays the bills. Plus, his dick does me justice. She was lost in the fantasy when she spotted Ito and Bert strolling into Porky Point as if they were walking down the runway of a fashion show.

Once Ito spotted her, he hurried her way with a Kool-Aid smile. "What's good, baby girl?" he extended his arms and forced a hug on her. "What's popping?" Ito repeated.

"Those crackers downtown are building a case on you two clowns. That trick Papo, the owner of the beer shop, is down there right now clapping his gums. It's safe to assume he's giving up tapes on shit they ain't even interested in." MaryLuz handed a white legal-sized envelope to Ito.

Ito tore it open and pulled out the ten-page statement of Lizzet Santiago. When he reached page three, his anger took over. "How the fuck I got caught up in this shit?" he asked as he read his name and then Bert's and Damaris's.

"If I were y'all two niggas, I'd lie low. As we speak, there's an asshole detective by the name of Ruiz who has a vicious hard-on for you," MaryLuz said, pointing to Bert.

"Me?" Bert asked, looking surprised.

"Yeah, you. And he's bringing all kinds of witnesses to build a homicide case against you. So I wouldn't be surprised if he gets a warrant on y'all's asses before the night is over. This shit is serious, li'l homie!"

Ito excused himself to go to the restroom, giving Bert an opportunity to mack on MaryLuz. MaryLuz welcomed the move. She was feeling horny. She had heard that Bert had a big dick and loved to freak out all the way. She looked him up and down, then slowly ran her tongue across her lips.

"What's up with you, bro? I been hearing a lot about you. These little hot-in-the-pants chickenheads been spitting your name out as if you were some kind of rap star," she said. She grabbed Bert's hand and sucked his middle finger.

"Damn! Dat's how you riding?" Bert grabbed his crotch and smiled. His dick instantly sprang to attention. He moved closer to her. He leaned back until he could see from all angles, making sure his partner in crime didn't creep up on him. Then he slid his hand between her legs. He slid his middle finger inside her to feel how wet she was. "Damn, ma! I'll get at you tonight!" he grunted. He removed his finger and sucked it, tasting her juices.

"You just make sure my people don't find out," MaryLuz said. She glanced toward the public restroom and saw Ito coming out.

"Don't worry about it. I need some of that good thing you got," Bert assured her as he nonchalantly slid back to his seat.

When Ito arrived at the table, he looked at MaryLuz and sensed that she wasn't happy being in a dingy spot like Porky Point and eating pork sandwiches. "Listen. Good looking on the info. We can handle the rest from here. Keep me updated on Papo," he said, passing the envelope to Bert.

"So who else is running their mouth besides bitch-ass Papo?" Bert asked.

"Like I said, there's no telling who's talking. All I know is y'all's names are popping up all over the place. Whatever y'all do, y'all ain't get that info from me, and get rid of it as soon as you use it," MaryLuz said. She extended her hand, waiting for her bonus and smiling charmingly.

Ito handed her a stack of $100 bills, and she blew him a kiss as she walked out of the Point and disappeared into the streets of North Philly.

Out on Franklin Street, Lizzet Santiago held a meeting on the corner with other drug addicts. "Yeah, po-po tried to put pressure on me to give them information, but y'all know me. I ride out for my people," she said as she directed her attention to Damaris. "Girl, they asked all kinds of questions about you, your son, the fine little nigga who be sticking to your son like glue . . . I mean, everybody!"

Whatever she said needed no clarification. Damaris knew this bitch was talking to the po-po. *Damn! She beat me to the punch!*

Damaris moved briskly up the sidewalk. She longed for a shot of dope, and her stomach was letting her know. Her shadow fell over the street like the specter of a forgotten thug. She looked for empty caps on the alley floor, hoping to find a couple of crumbs of crack. She was desperate, but she also knew that her chances were next to none of finding even a morsel.

Franklin Street had been a ghost town since the police started creeping around, holding all the drug pushers hostage in their homes. Damaris never imagined her life would become rearranged and turned inside out like the dirty panties she'd been wearing for a week straight.

Ito and Bert sat in front of 2630 North Franklin Street, waiting for their target. "This is it," Bert said.

"Yup." Ito leaned forward, peeking out the car window, observing the layout.

"Remember, everybody in the crib gets murked. No witnesses, no mess, in and out."

Ito was feeling a little nervous because it had been a while since he'd gone on a mission like this. He dug into the duffel bag and pulled out a Glock nine and a fitted cap. He slid leather gloves on and took a deep breath. "Ready, nigga?" he asked Bert. Bert shook his head.

Ito opened the car door and headed toward the house. He tried walking normal to blend in and not attract attention. He held the gun down by his side and kept an eye on his periphery.

At the front door, he took one long look up and down Franklin Street, making sure no witnesses were around. The streets were empty. Satisfied that he was alone, he knocked on the door.

"*Quien es?*" a female voice asked from behind the door.

"The gas meterman!" Ito responded, his adrenaline pumping. He could hear multiple locks being opened. He clutched his gun tighter.

The moment he and Bert saw the door crack open, they forced their way inside. The small woman was knocked down by the force of the door hitting her. The moment

Bert saw the woman he repeatedly pistol-whipped her. Ito scanned the room. It was clear. When he turned to Bert, he saw the woman was pregnant. He ran over and pushed Bert off of her.

"What the fuck?" Bert screamed.

"She pregnant." Ito pointed to the bloody woman holding her head to try to stop the bleeding.

Sobbing and trembling, the woman asked them, "*Porque?* Why? What you want?"

"Bitch, you know why we here!" Bert shouted, slapping her in the mouth so hard that her lip split open.

"Chill, nigga." Ito pushed Bert again.

"You push me one more time, I'ma light your ass up."

"Psst." Ito shook his head, but he didn't dare try to challenge Bert. Ito turned to the woman. "Listen. I'm going to ask you some questions. If you lie to me, my friend here is going to kill you. Understand me?" Ito stared into her eyes, letting her know this was no game. He grabbed her by the hair and moved her into the living room, where he duct-taped her hands behind her back and then her ankles.

She turned her head from side to side, terrified to no end. Ito felt sorry for the woman. He wished he didn't have to be there, but he knew he had to do what he had to do. "Who's in this house with you?" he asked.

"My two-year-old son. He's upstairs sleeping," the woman said.

"Yo, go check that out. I'll keep an eye out down here," Ito said.

Bert quietly walked up the stairs. His gun was pointed forward, ready to fire. He went room by room making sure no one was hiding. He looked in every closet, the bathroom, and bedrooms. The little boy was sleeping on the floor in his bedroom. Bert's first thought was to slump the kid. He aimed the gun straight at the boy's head. Right before pulling the trigger, the boy rolled over in his sleep. It startled Bert, but luckily he didn't fire the gun. This was Ito's mission, and he wasn't murdering no kid. If Ito wanted the kid dead, he could do it his damn self.

In a last attempt to save her and her son's life, the pregnant woman tried to loosen her hand enough to press the speed-dial button on her cell phone on the floor next to her. But Ito was too fast for her. "Bitch, I'll blow yo' brains all over this carpet if you try to get slick again!" he said. He taped her wrists securely, and then her mouth, strangling her sobs and pleas.

Bert came down the steps with his mask pulled down, revealing his face.

"What the fuck?" Ito said.

"What?" Bert asked.

"Your mask, nigga."

This sealed the fate of the young pregnant woman. Ito knew for sure they would have to slump her.

"Everything's clear. Little man's sleeping. Should I let him live or send him to hell with his *mami?*" he asked.

Ito just stared at him in disbelief. *Mothafucka's getting beside himself. Nigga lost his mind!*

The pregnant girl closed her eyes tightly.

"Nigga, you outta pocket, flashing your grill like that! This ho ain't supposed to see your face!" Ito knew it was only a matter of time before this episode came to an end.

"Stop the paranoia. We gonna slump this ho anyway," Bert said, staring at the trembling woman.

The woman opened her eyes wide and closed them. Her sobs gave Bert a hard-on. *Damn! I should get a shot of this hot, pregnant pussy.* He saw the way Ito was looking at him and remained calm.

Ito placed a pillow over the woman's head and fired a single shot into her skull. To ensure the job was completed, he fired another shot into her kidneys. He ransacked the living room to make it look like a robbery. He couldn't refrain from taking a small memento: her welfare ID card.

As they drove away from the scene, Ito inspected the papers MaryLuz had given him earlier that day, comparing the names on the ID welfare card to the name on the police statement. His heart pounded frantically when he realized the names weren't a match. "Damn! We slumped the wrong person!" he shouted. A tear escaped his eye as he pulled his cell phone out and dialed 911. "Hell! A pregnant woman was just shot in the head at 2630 North Franklin Street," he said.

Bert drove away in silence. They both had no problem putting in work and droppin' niggas who needed to get got, but this mistaken-identity shit was deeply emotional for them, especially seeing it was a pregnant woman with a child. They both realized they had taken this kid's family from him. They both knew what it was like growing up without parents. It was something they never wanted any kid to have to experience, and now they were the ones responsible.

They reached South Philly, where they abandoned the stolen car and destroyed the cell phone. "Man, what's done is done. It's too late to feel sorry. Shit happens," Bert said.

"Nigga, we killed the wrong person! That's not part of the game!" Ito thought about his own baby's mother.

Bert laughed coldly. "Bro, I'll holla at you in the a.m." He pulled away in his baby blue Lexus.

***

When the ambulance arrived at 2630 North Franklin Street, the paramedics found a little boy crying as he lay on top of his mother.

One of the paramedics felt for a pulse on the pregnant woman's wrist and found one. He shouted, "She's alive! Someone help me! She's alive! She's still alive!" The two paramedics picked Lucy Mendez's body up and placed her on a stretcher. They rushed her to Temple University Hospital, where doctors performed an emergency C-section to try to save the life of her unborn child.

It was a tense operating room. One set of doctors performed the C-section while the other set attempted to save Lucy's life. They were shuffling around each other, trying to perform their duties while staying out of the others' way. One team was successful. The other team wasn't.

With no one to claim the baby, the doctors named her Lucky. The bullet in Lucy's kidney had stopped two inches short of the infant's head.

Unfortunately, Lucy Mendez was not lucky. She died soon after the doctors removed the infant from her womb. She stayed alive long enough to birth her child. It was the ultimate sacrifice for her baby.

Chapter Seven

Payback Is a Bitch

Flip Kilos, Fat Angel, Bolo, D-Rock, Jay, and Shyla arrived at Isla Verde Restaurant shortly after midnight, ready to celebrate what was supposed to be Fat Angel's return to the drug game in Philly.

Inside the restaurant, Bolo tapped Jay on the shoulder. The salsa music was blaring from the speakers, so he had to yell. "Damn, kid! Look at that ass!" He pointed at a Puerto Rican chick who was leaning over the pool table.

"Yeah, that's a hustler's dream," Jay said, admiring the wide ass. When she turned her head to the side, Jay realized it was his shorty Lala's ass he was admiring.

The hostess escorted them to the VIP area, where they fed their nostrils, drank bottles of champagne, and discussed Fat Angel's future plans.

It was after two in the morning, and Flip Kilos was feeling good, flirting with the young hood rats who were plotting on his pockets. "Yo, kid, I'd love to smash that young thing there!" he said to Jay.

Jay walked over to Yari and surreptitiously handed her a wad of $100 bills and gave her a sign to handle her business. Jay went back to his table, raised his cup, and the others followed.

No one noticed the brown-skinned Mexican who was sitting two tables away until it was too late. Suddenly, gunfire erupted through the Isla Verde Restaurant, sending patrons scrambling for the exits as the gunman came eye to eye with his target.

D-Rock never had a chance to remove his TEC-9. The gunman aimed his Uzi and squeezed the trigger until the clip was empty. To make sure the job was complete, the gunman reached into D-Rock's waistband, pulled his TEC-9 out, and aimed it at D-Rock's already-motionless body slumped over the table. He squeezed the trigger until all sixteen bullets exploded in D-Rock's head.

Bolo crawled across the floor looking for an exit, not even thinking about helping his friend, D-Rock. He reached the front door just as Flip Kilos and Jay opened it and disappeared. The three of them were in Bolo's Jeep about to pull away when Bolo realized that Shyla wasn't with them. *She probably got shot.* He ordered Jay to speed away.

"Man, D-Rock is gone!" Fat Angel blared as he stared at Flip Kilos in obvious shock.

"Nigga, that's part of the game. You live by the gun, and you die by the gun. D-Rock is just another sorry-ass nigga lost to the drug game," Bolo said, firing up a blunt.

Flip Kilos and Angel just stared at Bolo in disbelief. They had aligned themselves with someone whose right-hand man had just been slumped, and all he could say was, "This is part of the game."

Fat Angel knew that most drug dealers were cold-blooded, but to hear Bolo vocalize it so callously made the hair on the back of his neck stand up.

Inside Bolo's house on Second and Ontario, Shyla sat shaking and confused. She had never been in a shoot-out before, let alone witnessed someone getting killed. Now she had experienced both. It was much different from what she had envisioned. It was nothing like in the movies.

Bolo had shown his true colors, leaving her in the restaurant in the middle of the gunfire, not bothering to even try to protect her. If it hadn't been for her own survival instincts, she would've been dead. She somehow escaped the violence as the gunman fired the Uzi semiautomatic recklessly. The bullets whizzed by her head as she scrambled across the floor. She crawled on her stomach the entire length of the restaurant, through spilled drinks, dropped purses, and shoes.

Why did that nigga leave me behind? she asked herself as she waited for Bolo and Fat Angel to return.

When Jay parked the Jeep in front of Bolo's house, Flip jumped out and disappeared into the night. Bolo noticed that the light was on in his living room, and he pulled his nine from his waistband. He approached the front door and put his ear to it. He couldn't hear anything, so he crouched down and snuck around to the window. When he peeked in, he saw Shyla sitting in the living room. He was taking no chances and held the nine until he was sure no one else was in the house.

He entered the house.

"Nigga, why the fuck did you leave me behind?" Shyla shouted.

Bolo stared at her as if she were crazy. "What you think, I was gonna wait for your trick ass?" He pushed her away.

"You dirty nigga! You're just like all the other niggas out here! You only care about yourself!"

Her words cut so deep into Bolo that he pistol-whipped Shyla, splitting her head open and sending her charging to the floor.

Fat Angel looked on helplessly, not knowing what to do. This shit was way more drama than he could handle.

"Nigga, you a coward! You shoulda pistol-whipped the Puerto Rican kid who was trying to blow your dumb ass away!"

Bolo snapped. He kicked her in the face and neck.

She pleaded, "Bolo, I'm sorry!" But her pleas weren't enough to stop him from stomping her entire body until she convulsed.

"Bitch, I'll kill you up in this mothafucka! Don't ever disrespect me!" He knelt down and beat her with the pistol several times, knocking three of her front teeth out.

Shyla lay on the floor unconscious, her head in a puddle of blood as Bolo stood over her. She'd survived a shootout, but she might not survive a beating from Bolo. It was the life she chose. The money and lifestyle were too much for her to resist.

"Bitch, you make me sick!" he said, staring at Fat Angel and Jay for their reactions as he pulled his dick out and pissed in her face.

"Man, you gave her a hell of a beating!" Fat Angel said. "I hope the fuck she's still alive." The last thing Angel needed was to be implicated in a senseless murder.

"Some bitches need to have their asses whipped. The trick had it coming anyway," Bolo said, feeling somehow vindicated.

Shyla's face looked like a swollen plum as she lay on the floor motionless. She awoke from her ass whipping and sat up against the wall still in tremendous pain, the blood pouring out of her mouth from a cut inside her upper lip. Her face felt like it had a heart of its own. Her right eye was completely shut, and a five-inch cut decorated the side of her head. She thought about calling a cab to take her to the hospital, but in doing so, she would have to file a police report. So against her better judgment, she stood up and walked to the bathroom to clean herself up.

Looking at herself in the mirror, she couldn't believe what she saw. Her face was rearranged into something she didn't recognize. Her face looked worse than Tina Turner's after Ike beat her ass with her own spiked high-heeled shoe in the back of a limo.

Shyla was furious and hurt. *Fuck that little-dick nigga!* She decided to teach Bolo a lesson. Some major shit was about to jump off. "Fuck that animal!" she screamed as tears rolled down her face.

She went back into the living room and fumbled through some clothes on the floor until she found her phone. She dialed the number of the FBI in the City of Brotherly Love. She had looked the number up two days ago.

"Federal Bureau of Investigation. Special Agent Cleary speaking. How may I help you?"

"My name is Shyla, and I have information on a drug house."

"What is the location, and who's running it?" Agent Cleary asked.

"Well, his street name is Bolo. The drug house is at 3067 North Indiana Avenue," Shyla said eagerly.

"Do you know what kind of drugs are in the house and how much?" Agent Cleary asked.

"Somewhere between five and twenty kilos of crack. Oh, he's driving a dark green Jeep," Shyla said. With that, she hung up the phone so her number couldn't be traced.

Bolo and Fat Angel got out of the Jeep and hurried up to the apartment that Flip Kilos had set up to be their new stash house. They banged on the door and yelled, "Titi! Titi!"

"What's going on, *papi?*" Titi asked as she opened the door, giving Fat Angel a kiss on the lips.

The light in the room was dim, making it impossible for Bolo to see into the back room. Except for a table in the middle of the room, there was no furniture, which seemed strange to him. There were several stacks of kilos on the table.

A tall Dominican man appeared from the rear of the apartment. Fat Angel recognized him, as they had recently met. Angel knew him by his street name, Flaco. The man's smile made Fat Angel feel uneasy.

Flaco turned around and spoke to a younger Dominican who had positioned himself in the far corner of the room. While Angel's heart pounded forcefully in his chest, he remained expressionless.

"What can we do for you?" Flaco asked in a friendly tone.

"Flip instructed us to come here. He said you knew what to do," Fat Angel said.

"Yeah. Allow me to confer with my associates." Flaco disappeared into the back room while Bolo and Angel remained under the scrutiny of the young Dominican.

Five minutes passed before Flaco walked back into the room. "You looking to cop right now?"

"Nah, we're here to arrange how we're gonna run this shit," Fat Angel said impatiently.

"Shit, man! We have no idea why Flip sent you here. However, we have no problems supplying you with what you need." Flaco was following his script to a T. Flip had instructed him to test Bolo's and Angel's hearts, but unbeknownst to him, Flip didn't expect Bolo and Angel to react with deadly results.

Flaco's words confirmed Angel's first impression. They were going to have to shoot their way out.

In one quick motion, Bolo reached under his Sean John sweatshirt, pulled out his TEC-9, and got the drop on the Dominican kid standing by the door. He squeezed the trigger. Through the flash and gun smoke, Bolo watched his target crawling on the floor. Aiming for the kill, he leveled his gun to the face of the Dominican and plastered his face to the floor. Bolo then turned to Flaco, who was trying to slide through a side window. But he was too slow.

Now it was time to get out. Bolo stepped over Flaco's body and went out the window, landing in a garbage-strewn yard. "Let's get the fuck out of here!" he shouted.

Fat Angel was breathing hard as the two of them ran from the scene. All the while, Bolo was firing his gun blindly over his shoulder. By the time they spotted Jay parked at the intersection ahead of them, Bolo was out of bullets, and Fat Angel was out of breath.

In a house a block behind them, 2-year-old Kassandra Ortiz was sleeping next to her mother. Hearing gunfire was an everyday thing in North Philly. People rarely looked to see where the shots were coming from. Kassandra was hugging the teddy bear her grandmother had given her a week ago for her second birthday. Her mother never heard the thud of the bullet as it came through the wall. The two lay restfully next to one another.

Blood gushed out of Kassandra's neck like a pump.

Chapter Eight

I Heard It Through the Grapevine

Lil' Bert was nearing his baby mom's crib at Fourth and Cayuga when his cell phone chirped. "Holla at ya boy," he answered while parking his Lexus in front of his baby's mother's crib.

"What's up, *papi?* You stood me up last night," said MaryLuz, obviously upset.

"Baby girl, something came up. I'll be there around six."

"Okay. I'm staying at 2539 North Marshall Street. I'll be waiting," MaryLuz said.

Later, when Bert pulled up to MaryLuz's crib, he turned the motor off and lit up a blunt. He was a half hour early, and he didn't want her to think he was too eager.

When he finished the blunt, he got out of the car and walked into a Spanish bodega to pass time. No sooner was he inside than he heard the bodega clerk speaking about a shooting that had taken place at the Isla Verde restaurant. Bert had noticed the flowers up on Indiana Avenue when he drove by, but he'd paid it no mind until now.

"Some cats from Brick City, New Jersey, ran up in that joint and lit that trifling-ass D-Rock up! That's what all those sorry-ass drug dealers should all get!" the bodega clerk said in a bitter tone, looking Bert up and down.

Damn girl's crazy! Bert thought. He purchased a can of whipped cream and a bottle of vodka and walked out of the store.

He knocked on MaryLuz's door, and when she opened it, he could hardly contain himself. She was wearing a white transparent Victoria's Secret nightie. Bert wiped the sweat from his brow and said, "Damn, ma! You got a fat ass!" He grabbed her firm buttocks and squeezed.

"Can you handle this?" MaryLuz asked, motioning for him to come inside. She led him to the basement, where a king-size bed and mirrors on every wall awaited them. "I like it hard and rough. Slap me and pull my hair," she said.

Bert was more than willing to comply with her wishes. He threw her on the bed, snatched her panties to the side, and held her open for a few seconds. "Damn, ma! You bring the freak out in me!" he said, spreading whipped cream down the crack of her delicious ass.

"Come on, nigga! Stop playing, and ram that in my ass!" MaryLuz needed to be punished in a dirty way. The more Bert slapped and pumped her thick ass, the louder her moans got. She bit her bottom lip until Bert came deep inside her bowels.

"I told you my shit was good. Are you spending the night?" MaryLuz asked. She fell back on the bed and spread her thighs.

Before Bert could answer, his cell phone went off. "What?" he said, annoyed to no end.

"Where are you, nigga? I've been waiting on you all day!" Ito said angrily.

"I'm taking care of business," Bert replied. He pulled MaryLuz's head down to his throbbing dick and placed the receiver next to her mouth so Ito could hear her slurping away on his manhood.

"Yo, get at me when you're done," Ito said.

Bert dropped the phone onto the bed just when he gushed a load deep into MaryLuz's throat. They made freaky love all night and through the morning. Then MaryLuz gave Bert the 411 on every major nigga who was on the come-up. She also told him all about Fat Angel and his new crew.

The pieces of the puzzle were coming together for Bert. *No wonder Fat Angel hasn't been around in a minute,* he thought and laughed out loud.

"I'm telling you, *papi,* they lit D-Rock up like a Christmas tree! I saw the crime scene photos up in homicide." MaryLuz sat with her legs crossed. She was excited to see Bert in an obvious trance.

Bert continued to think in silence, his hands folded against the pillow. *So Fat Angel's trying to cut in on my chips, is he?*

"What's wrong, *papi?*" MaryLuz asked as she kissed his neck.

Bert pushed her back on the bed and sucked her pussy until she came. Then he got dressed and left her crib. *Time to get back to business.*

Chapter Nine

Coldhearted

Lil' Bert drove to Hancock and Cambria Streets, spotting Three Finger June standing outside his crib. Bert pulled over and motioned for June to get in the car.

June got in and almost sat on the AK-47 that was lying on the seat. "Damn, dawg! Shit is hot out here!" June said hesitantly. He looked Bert dead in the eyes.

"Nigga, I heard Fat Angel's trying to cut into us," Bert said.

"Yeah. Word on the street is preacher boy down Franklin Street's backing his whole connect," Three Finger June said.

"Yo, I just heard what they did to that nut-ass nigga D-Rock," Bert said as the duo headed over to Ito's place.

On the corner of Pike Street, Three Finger June saw Pretty Tone, Fat Angel's stepson, talking to two street girls. "Yo, dat kid is worth about a hundred thousand. He's the nigga pushing dat purple haze weed all over North," he said and rolled down the window. "What's popping, kid?" June hollered, pulling his hat down over his eyebrows.

Pretty Tone walked over to the car. "Yo, you trying to cop? What you need?"

June and Bert got out of the car, and the two girls instinctively walked away. They could sense some bad intentions coming from the two men in the car.

"Your time is up, little homie!" Bert said sternly. He opened the trunk and signaled for Pretty Tone to get in.

Pretty Tone pleaded, "Man, I don't wanna die! I just want to eat like everybody else!"

"Nigga, hop in or die here!" Bert said, holding on to Pretty Tone's arm and pointing his gun at his heart. Bert smacked him in the face with the side of the gun, and Tone fell sideways into the trunk.

They drove to an empty warehouse on Butler Street. When the trunk opened, Tone was curled up in the fetal position and crying like a baby.

"Get out!" Bert yelled, cocking his gun.

Pretty Tone got out and dropped to his knees, pleading for his life. "Please don't kill me! I'll do anything you want! I don't want to die!"

Bert didn't give a fuck about this nigga's tears. *This boy's a bitch!* he thought as he grew angrier by the second. The last thing Lil' Bert wanted to see was a so-called gangster crying like a bitch. That shit drove him up the wall. "Bitch-ass nigga, I got a few questions. You answer them, and I might spare your life. Tell me where you rest your head at night." Bert put his AK-47 under Pretty Tone's nose.

"I stay down on Sixth and Bristol with my mom and pop!" Tone said, and his bowels broke. Shit filled his underpants and dripped down his leg.

"Is your pop back in the game?" Bert asked.

"I don't know dude's business. I don't fuck with him like dat," Pretty Tone answered.

Bert squeezed the trigger and held it, emptying the whole clip into Pretty Tone's body. Then he went through his pockets, taking all his cash and dope.

Bert and Three Finger June drove to Sixth and Bristol and ransacked Pretty Tone's mother's house until they found a shoebox containing $55,000 and a bag of fake jewels. Before they left, both of them set separate fires.

"Yo, I'll get at you later. Take the cash with you," Bert said after dropping him off in front of his crib on Hancock and Cambria.

It was Bert's duty to live his life coldheartedly. He never cared too much about anyone. He slept well at night, but ever since his little argument with Ito, his conscience was eating at him at night.

Chapter Ten

The Great Bust

Detective Cruz and his partner, Detective Angela Dash, waited in their unmarked car a block away from Indiana and Glenwood Avenues, watching and monitoring the addicts and hustlers coming and going. Cruz and Dash were locals from the Twenty-fifth District, and they were helping the "big boys."

"Cruz, there's the dark green Jeep. Get on their tail," Detective Dash said, pointing to the Jeep. Detective Dash wrote down the license plate number and ran it, hoping for a reason to stop it.

Bolo and Angel had no clue they were being followed. The detectives trailed them for three hours, taking pictures with a digital camera at every location they frequented. They were on camera exchanging money, drugs, and guns. Over the course of three hours, they had obtained enough evidence to make an arrest and seek a search warrant.

"These are the drug dealers of today, so sloppy and unaware," Detective Dash said as she lit up a cigarette. She added, "We're on to something big here. I know these drug dealers."

Detective Cruz sat quietly while he fantasized about his next vacation and the fat raise this bust was sure to bring. "One more transaction and we can bust these slimeballs and put them away for a long time," he said, rolling down the window of the unmarked car and taking another picture. These drug dealers were so stupid, the cops weren't worried they'd be spotted.

Agent Cleary sat in his Center City office, waiting for the search warrant to come back from the main office in Washington, D.C. He stared at his fax machine, thinking that this was the big bust. His unit hadn't had a major bust in over three years, and the pressure was beginning to get to him. This bust could put the spotlight back on his unit.

When he saw the red light beep on, he jumped up from his chair and said, "It's here!" The other FBI agents involved in the Safe Street task force gathered around. Agent Cleary grabbed the search warrant for the 2967 North Indiana Avenue location, and then another one for 3069 North Hutchinson Street. Then he picked up his cell phone and called Detectives Cruz and Dash.

"Hello," Detective Dash answered, smiling.

"We have the warrants for both locations. Tomorrow morning, we'll pay these little dealers a visit. My unit will assist you in raiding both spots. So wrap it up for today. Thank you for helping out," Cleary said and hung up the cell phone.

"It's on for tomorrow morning. Warrants came through," Detective Dash said to Cruz. "We're done for today. Let's go back to the station."

When they arrived at the Twenty-fifth District, she got out of the car with all the notes she had been jotting down and told her partner, "I'll see you in the morning." She slammed the car door. As she bent over, she gave Detective Cruz a peek at her perfectly shaped ass as she disappeared into the station.

Chapter Eleven

Snitching Ain't Easy

Detectives Cruz and Dash waited to see who they'd been assigned to assist.

Chief Jackson motioned for them to come into his office. "This is Agent Cleary," Chief Jackson said. "He's in charge of this bust today. He will instruct you both on the roles you are to play. Please don't fuck this up." He stared at Dash and Cruz.

"Don't worry, we won't. We want these assholes off the streets as much as you do," Detective Dash said.

The FBI agent left the Twenty-fifth District with Detectives Dash and Cruz tagging along. They got into separate cars. Dash, Cleary, Stevens, Woods, and MacGregor drove to 2967 North Indiana Avenue. They were wearing blue jackets with big yellow FBI letters on their backs and bulletproof vests underneath. Once they arrived at the Indiana Avenue location, they parked in front of 2967 and spoke on their cell phones.

A block down, Detective Cruz, along with FBI agents Santo, Major, Quin, and Callahan, waited for the signal.

Inside the house, Fat Angel lay in bed with a young whore named Carmen, getting his freak on.

"*Sí, papi,* I saw those two dudes take Pretty Tone for a ride," Carmen told Angel as she wiped the sweat and cum dripping from the crack of her ass.

"Here's another hundred," Angel said. "Pick me up a prepaid phone at the corner store and a box of blunts."

Carmen got dressed and walked out the door in plain view of the FBI. Before she took three steps, agents quietly snatched her up and shoved her in the back seat of an unmarked car.

"Who's in the house?" Cleary asked Carmen.

"I don't know." Carmen pursed her lips defiantly.

"You'd better tell me who the fuck is in there, or you're getting the rap for anything we find in there."

"I don't know nothin' about nothin' in that house. I was meetin' my girl and went in the wrong house. Some nigga named Fat Angel in there."

"Green light!" Agent Cleary said into his walkie-talkie, giving the signal to start the raid.

At that very moment, Fat Angel was turning two kilos of powder cocaine into crack. *Damn, I'm good!* he thought as he violated one of the major rules of the game: not getting high on his own shit. He placed a large rock into the pipe and took another hit just as the FBI burst through the front door.

"FBI! Get down on the floor!" Agent Cleary yelled, pointing his semiautomatic handgun at Angel's head.

Detectives Dash and MacGregor searched the house while Agent Stevens read Fat Angel his rights. Fat Angel lay on the bedroom floor with tears flowing down his face. He knew he was history. The only thing he could say was, "Life, nigga! Life! They gonna give you life!"

"Who owns this house?" Dash asked as she held up two of the eight kilos she found.

"I'll only talk to the dealmaker," Angel said as Agent Cleary handcuffed him.

When the search was over, the detectives and agents fled the house carrying bags of evidence.

A crowd had gathered in front of the address. Shyla stood among the spectators, smiling. "That little-dick nigga is going down!" she said to no one in particular as she watched the detectives escorting Fat Angel to the unmarked car.

When they arrived at FBI headquarters, Angel asked for a deal even before he was fingerprinted and photographed. Agent Cleary couldn't believe his luck.

"Listen, I'll give you the big man, but I want a deal. I'm just a small fry. I'm not the one you want," Angel said, looking hard at Agent Cleary.

"Mr. Cruz, we can play games, or we can serve each other well. I ask the questions, and you give the answers. Do you understand me?" Cleary said in a friendly tone.

"I can only tell you what I know," Angel responded, still not comprehending that he was about to become a snitch.

"That's all I want—the correct answers. And if you lie, my friend, I will stick you with every unsolved murder in the city. Now, two weeks ago, a young drug dealer was kidnapped on Indiana Avenue right down the block from your residence. He turned up dead. We know he was your stepson. Tell me who did it," Cleary said, offering Angel a cigarette.

Fat Angel waved him off. "Yeah, I have an idea who did it, but before I say anything, I want to talk to a lawyer. I do have some rights, don't I?" Angel said. He knew he was in deep shit, and he might as well cut himself a deal from the door.

"Do you know these guys?" Agent Cleary asked. He pushed Flip Kilos's and Bolo's pictures across the table.

"I will talk to you when I have a lawyer present," Angel repeated.

"Okay, prepare yourself. You're about to get arraigned," Agent Cleary said.

The judge read Fat Angel the charges he was facing. She asked him if he needed a lawyer and informed him he would remain in custody until the trial. Since he was on federal parole and had prior convictions, the judge considered him a flight risk.

Angel was trembling. He could see he was in deep shit. The thought of being locked up for a max bid was terrifying.

Once he was back in the holding cell, Agent Cleary appeared at the cell door. "Are you ready to see your court-appointed lawyer?

These crackers are trying to bury me alive, Angel thought as the agent escorted him to the interview room.

"Mr. Cruz, come in," said a tall, middle-aged, sharp-dressed white man. "My name is Charles Fibre. I'll be representing you. I want to be completely clear with you. You are facing some heavy charges. Should you decide to cooperate, I may be able to save you from multiple life sentences. They are indicting you under the RICO Act. The federal sentencing guidelines require you to be sentenced to life for five hundred grams of cocaine and crack, and according to the indictment, they confiscated eight kilos in total. Since you're a convicted felon, you fall under those federal sentencing guidelines," he said, pointing to the chart he had laid on the table.

The words "Life, nigga!" popped out of the chart.

Attorney Fibre knew he had Angel's undivided attention. "They're building a high-profile case against you and your codefendants. When they catch up with them, there's no doubt in my mind they're going to give you up. I've been in this business for twenty-five years, and I've seen the biggest and baddest tough guys flip in a matter of seconds when they hear the words 'life sentence' whispered in their ears. Now are you going to ride this thing out like a true gangster, or are you going to cooperate? Time is running out, and right now you control your own destiny." Mr. Fibre remained silent long enough for his words to take hold.

Angel sat back in his chair and thought about how he had stayed true to the game while everyone around him had gotten rich. He thought about how Flip Kilos had crossed him, costing him fifteen years of his life in the federal system. He thought about Bolo and how he had tried to play him like a sucka by treating him like a nobody.

Fuck this! "I ain't going back to prison. Who do I talk to? I want my deal in black and white. I'll give them what they want, but I go home. That's the only way I'll talk. Since you're my lawyer, you can deliver that message to the trash on the other side of the window," he said, pointing at the one-way mirror, although he really didn't know if the FBI agent was watching him.

Chapter Twelve

G-Ford

It was a dog-day afternoon at the State Correctional Institution–Graterford, where Big Boy, Little G, King Unknown, Ill Dee, and Black Manny had spent the last five years of their lives on a drug case.

Graterford Prison was a maximum-security joint located right outside of Philadelphia. It was considered the worst of the worst prisons in the state. Inmates were housed in six-by-thirteen cells on cellblocks that were a football field and a half long. Security cameras and corrupt COs who were always looking to make a few extra dollars watched over them. Fights, stabbings, illegal gambling, rape, and murder were the order of the day.

Some inmates chose to do their bids and go home. Others viewed Graterford as a hustler's dream, a place where they could stack cash while they did their time.

To the Suicidal Riders, G-Ford, as it was called, was nothing but a moneymaking enterprise, providing opportunities to those in the crew with family members or close friends doing time. Hands down, the Suicidal Riders ran G-Ford. Anyone from Franklin Street who came through the prison was automatically taken care of, and if a nigga didn't want to play his part, he was fed to the wolves.

Having control of the prison underworld allowed the Suicidal Riders and Lil' Bert to gain firsthand information on niggas from different parts of the city who were plotting against them. Dudes who wanted to fit in with the movers and shakers of the jail talked too much about what they were going to do when they hit the streets again and what their people and homies were doing.

Since gossip traveled quickly in prison, Jaw Bone was filled with excitement when Vicky, his cousin, told him over the phone that their older cousin, Flip Kilos, was jumping back into the drug game and declaring war on some heavyweight Puerto Rican cats from Franklin Street. Jaw Bone saw himself becoming the drug dealer he always wanted to be.

For eleven years, Jaw Bone had been branded a rat, trading information on inmates for packs of Newports. Word around the state prisons was that in addition to being a rat, he ate a mean dick, thus the nickname Jaw Bone.

He hated the fact that all the niggas from the Franklin Street Suicidal Riders had the jail on lock with gambling tables, cell phones, cash money, cigarettes, and the right guards on their payroll. They also had the place flooded with heroin, crack, and weed. Female correctional officers knew that if they provided just a few niggas with a quick shot of pussy, they could get paid daily, and they did.

The guards who lived in the hood smuggled drug packages into the institution for quick money. Some of them were street hustlers themselves, and getting paid was the only thing that mattered to them. Besides, if they didn't get theirs, some of the white ho guards would. Hell, most of them sucked and fucked for free! Niggas on lockdown wanted to be up in these females' faces, flossing and shooting game at them, so why not get paid for it?

"Game is to be sold, not told," Correctional Officer Jackie Delsmith told the new rookie she was training as she pointed down the back of C-block at 480 lustful eyes. "That shit they teach you in Elizabethtown is bullshit! It doesn't work here. This is Graterford! These guys will come at you from all angles, and if you act like a bitch, they will treat you like one. Remember this: pussy is what's gonna keep you safe, not these crackpot white boy COs." She was giving Officer Temeka Jackson the lowdown, a dose of penitentiary reality.

When the noon count arrived, Delsmith showed CO Jackson what inmates did with their time. "Count time! Count time! Lights on. ID in hands!" Officer Delsmith, better known on C-Block as Dee, shouted over the bullhorn.

As she walked down the B-2 section with her clipboard, shaking her ass, Black Manny stood over his toilet pissing, wearing only his boxers. When Dee and CO Jackson reached his cell, Dee stopped, stared with lust, and licked her lips, remembering the time when she intentionally bumped into him as he was coming out of the shower. "Get used to it," she told CO Jackson, as the new CO stared too, but in shock.

Ms. Jackie Delsmith was a 32-year-old single mother. She was a brown-skinned, jazzy sister who was five feet four inches tall. She came to work wearing a different wig each day and pretty, fake nails. Her little frame and nice fat ass, along with her perky set of breasts, made her quite sexy. She was the epitome of ghetto ho-dom.

After count was over, Dee was waiting for Black Manny. "Manny! Black Manny! Come here!" she shouted as Black Manny walked down the steps toward the side yard.

Manny made his way toward the C-block bridge, where Dee was sitting at the desk, supposedly monitoring the men walking up and down the tiers. "What's up, Dee?"

he asked, looking her up and down and not caring who was watching. Shortening the distance between them, he leaned over and said, "Damn, ma! When are you gonna bless a Puerto Rican nigga with some of that brown sugar?" Black Manny spoke with such cockiness that there was no question about who was running shit on C-block.

Damn! That Rican nigga is too much for one bitch. Makes me want to get with him in front of the whole cellblock, Dee thought as she watched Black Manny strutting off to the side yard.

When he returned after yard was over, he ran into Dee at the bridge. She was looking fresh and delicious. "What's up, Dee? You working overtime, huh?" he asked.

"Yeah, I got bills to pay," Dee answered.

Black Manny watched her lips shape around the soda bottle she placed to her mouth. She ran her tongue around the opening of the bottle, then licked her lips. She knew what she was doing. She smiled, then repeated her subtle seduction.

After count, Dee opened Black Manny's cell door and said, "I need you to help me take the trash to the back dock." As she spoke, her eyes were riveted by Manny's groin.

Although he wasn't a block worker, Manny welcomed the opportunity to be out of his cell.

When they reached the back dock where the trash dumpster was located, Dee waited until Manny had thrown the last bag of trash into the dumpster. Then she led him into the property room. She kissed him hard and deeply while undoing her uniform, dropping her pants to her ankles. She got on her knees and pulled Manny's pants down, taking his swollen dick head into her mouth. When she tasted his cum, she pulled his dick out of her mouth and lustfully said, "We don't have a lot of time. I want you to fuck me doggie style, *papi!*"

Manny quickly followed her orders. When he slid inside her, he took her breath away. He grabbed her by her hair, forgetting she had a wig on, and pulled it off.

"Oooooh! Ooh, shiiitt, I'm ready to cum!" Dee squealed.

Black was busting too. He came so hard inside her that he could feel it dripping out of her. He pulled out and slapped his dick stick against her ass cheeks, spreading what cum was left over her ass. "Damn! I want some of this ass!" he said, sliding two fingers into her moist anus.

She squeezed her ass tightly, then pulled away from him. "That fuck was worth a ho losing her job. Next time I'll treat you to some of this booty," Dee said as she put her wig back on.

From that day on, Dee became the property of the Suicidal Riders. She smuggled in drugs, cell phones, and whatever other contraband they wanted. She thought she was playing Black Manny for the little bit of cash he was laying on her, but in reality she was nothing but a gullible bitch who had solidified her position as a whore to be used and discarded.

When the sun went down, G-Ford turned into a city of open vice. Everyone was into something, whether it was legal or not, and hardly anyone gave a damn.

The Suicidal Riders were flying high, raking in the cash from every angle—loan sharking, drugs, extortion, and gambling. This was their society, their community, and they were regarded as pariahs. In Graterford, they ruled C-block and dictated who was who and what was right and what was wrong. They ran the joint according to their own brand of morality. This was the citadel of convicted felons and hardened criminals, men who took lives simply because they could.

It was a bustling C-block that found Jaw Bone playing cards at the poker table in the rear of the block. At a little past seven, the Suicidal Riders were plotting on Jaw Bone.

"Dig, man. I'm saying that nigga's gotta get knocked tonight. Dee is on, so no one's got to stand for count," King Unknown said, pointing toward the table where Jaw Bone was sitting. "We got the green light from Bert. Shit's got to be handled. No rap!"

"Yeah, let's do it," Big Boy said while emptying a bag of chips into his mouth.

"Uh-huh, all right. Let's get down," Little G said and pulled a rusty guitar string from his pocket.

"Man, listen. Go holler at dude. Tell him Little G wants to talk to him. Then you be the lookout," Black Manny said.

Little G listened attentively.

Big Boy walked over to the card table and tapped Jaw Bone on the shoulder. "Listen, Little G needs to holler at you. He's waiting up by your hut," he said.

Jaw Bone started to say something, but when he realized who it was, he checked his chips in and walked to his cell. When he got there, he saw the Suicidal Riders spread out across the top tier. He entered his cell, B2-048, and Little G was sitting on the bunk.

"Nigga, you got my paper?" Little G asked, pushing up on Jaw Bone.

"Man, I'm waiting on a package my cousin's gonna send me. I got you, son!" Jaw Bone said, hoping Little G would cut him some slack.

"Nah, nigga. I waited too long. In fact, I want some juice on that," Little G said. He shut the cell door, pulled the curtain, and then pulled out his dick. "And you better swallow my nut!"

As Jaw Bone got on his knees and prepared to suck Little G's dick, Black Manny crept into the cell with the guitar string in his hands and quickly placed it around Jaw Bone's neck. He pulled the wire hard and held it there with a death grip. When he saw Jaw Bone's eyes roll to the back of his head, he pulled harder to ensure the dick eater was dead. When he let up on the wire, yellow mucus poured out of Jaw Bone's mouth.

Black Manny and Little G lifted Jaw Bone off the floor and laid him on his bunk and turned the TV on to create the appearance that he was asleep. As they were about to bounce, Black Manny turned around and instructed Big Boy to go retrieve a rat trap from the back of the block.

Big Boy didn't waste any time, and when he returned minutes later, he stood there dumbfounded and amazed as he watched Black Manny remove the rat from the trap and shove it up Jaw Bone's ass.

"Suicidal Riders for life!" Big Boy said, removing the latex gloves and flushing them down the toilet. They walked out of the cell as nonchalantly as they arrived.

When Officer Delsmith finished her evening count, securing the cell doors and counting each man, she hadn't noticed that inmate Raymond "Jaw Bone" Santos was dead.

The next morning, no one missed Jaw Bone when he failed to show up for work in the prison clothing industry. The C-block guards went about their daily routines, doing their morning and afternoon counts. It wasn't until the mailroom officer sent for Jaw Bone to hand him a certified letter from the court that they discovered him stinking and dead in his bed.

An immediate lockdown of C-block was ordered. The lockdown lasted for ten days. Security and a state police detective interviewed every inmate on C-block, but just like on the streets, no one had seen or heard anything.

Jaw Bone's murder went unsolved. He wasn't worth the time and hours it would take to investigate who had done the State a favor. After all, he was just another punk looking for a quick come-up.

Chapter Thirteen

The Agony of Defeat

Correctional Officer Jackie Delsmith sat in her car contemplating how she had allowed herself to get caught up in such a dangerous game. She wiped the tears from her cheeks and stared suspiciously at the man she'd been hearing so much about ever since she'd started fucking Black Manny in Graterford Prison.

Dee got out of her car and into Bert's car. "Hello," she said, smiling coyly. Bert looked good, and she couldn't deny it.

"I'm here to drop off a gift Black Manny wants you to have," Bert said coldly.

"What gift?" Dee asked, her eyes brightening as she looked at him.

Black Manny had already put Bert down with Dee's activities. Lately though, Dee started acting as if she wasn't with the program. Manny decided to bring her back into the fold by having the big boss himself pay her a visit.

Dee was getting more curious by the second to see the gift Manny had bought her. She tried to justify her involvement with the Suicidal Riders as a way of getting back at her ex-boyfriend, Lieutenant Tyrone Brooks, for dumping her funky ass for the shift commander's 17-year-old daughter who was hot between the legs. Afterward, she vowed to fuck every inmate she desired.

Lieutenant Brooks knew all about Dee's activities, but he looked the other way because his career was already on the line. Lieutenant Brooks was one of the shift commander's most trusted lieutenants, and if he ever found out that the lieutenant was fucking his daughter, he'd have his job.

Dee was nervous and anxious to see the gift Black Manny had for her. When Bert reached under his seat and pulled out a .45 and placed it on his lap, suddenly she was afraid she was going to die. There was no gift. This was all about her refusal to be Manny and the Suicidal Riders' mule, and Bert was here to apply the pressure.

Bert read her the riot act. Fear erupted inside Dee like a violent storm as he spoke. "Listen, you slut! You've been paid too healthy to start acting like a goody-two-shoes ho. Now I want you to see the gift my nigga has for you," he said. He reached inside the glove compartment and pulled out a cell phone. He flipped it open to reveal the photo of Dee sucking Black Manny's dick. Bert pushed a button, and the next photo was of Dee's three children.

The cell phone was the same one she had smuggled into the prison for Manny. She suddenly knew she'd been played in her own game. "Please don't do this to me!" she begged.

"If any of my niggas gets so much as a dirty look from you or any of your coworkers, I know where you lay your head at night. And if any of my niggas end up in the hole, I'ma beat your ass down! And one more thing. If any of my niggas want to wet their dick, you serve them! Understand me? 'Cause if you don't, you will pay with your life. Act like you got some sense, and I'll see to it that you are taken care of at all times."

Dee lowered her head and started to cry. "Yeah," she said. "I understand you."

"Now get your stinking ass out of my car before I cap your wig back, bitch! Maybe next time I'll let you have some of this Puerto Rican dick," Bert said as Dee got out of the car.

Dee sat in her car and cried for a long time, not knowing what to do. She thought about reporting Manny and his crew to prison officials, but at the same time she thought about her future. She needed her job to survive.

Dee spent her three days off figuring out a way to tell Black Manny she was pregnant with his child—at least, she was relatively sure it was his. She was confused. For as far as she knew, it could belong to any of the niggas in Graterford she had been fucking around with. She thought about getting an abortion, but she was thrilled at the idea of having a curly-haired Puerto Rican kid.

When Dee returned to the prison, she was dumbfounded to see Black Manny walking toward the C-block bridge with a box in his hand, wearing a smile from ear to ear. "What's going on, Manny?" she asked in a low voice. Even though he had dogged her, she knew she was in love with him.

"You tell me. What's popping?" Manny replied.

"Why do you have your things packed up?"

"I'm going home! I max out today! Don't worry, I'll be in touch."

Dee's legs were weak, and her mind was in a scramble to make sense of what Manny had just told her. She felt lonely and shameful. "Home?" she snapped.

"Yes, home! Which part of 'home' do you not understand?" Manny said. He ordered her to write him a pass to the assessment unit, where they were waiting to process him out of the prison.

"Manny, I'm pregnant!" Dee said. She studied his face for any kind of sign.

"It's not mine! Shit! Who hasn't fucked you in this place? Bitch, I'll see you on the other side of these walls. Remember, take care of my niggas. Holler at your boy!" He snatched the pass out of Dee's hand and walked off the block toward his freedom.

In the parking lot of the prison, Lil' Bert waited anxiously in a white BMW limo. He wanted Black Manny to leave prison in style. After all, he was to replace Ito in the Suicidal Riders drug gang.

Chapter Fourteen

"You Ain't Never Lied"

Flip Kilos and Bolo smiled almost simultaneously. Just recently they had discovered they had more in common than just drug dealing. As they opened up to each other, sharing personal stories of their lives, they both realized they shared the same sexual tastes. They each liked a finger in their ass while getting sucked. Although Flip Kilos wouldn't admit it, he let his girl stuff a dildo up his ass.

"This is crazy, man! I feel like I've known you all my life!" Bolo said as he looked around Flip Kilos's office.

"Believe me, I'll make it worth your while. Half of everything we make and a lifetime supply of top-quality heroin." He punctuated his words by pulling out a kilo of pure *manteca* and slapping it down on top of his desk.

"Damn, man! This is where the money's at!" Bolo took the kilo in his hands and held it firmly.

"Young buck, I could make you rich in no time, but you must prove yourself to me. How far are you willing to go for this paper?" Flip Kilos asked.

Bolo rubbed his sweaty palm down the side of his leg. "Man, I'll do whatever it takes. I'm hungry! I want this shit bad! I want the hustler's dream—money, bitches, and power!" Bolo expected more than the blank stare Flip was giving him.

Flip would have never recruited Bolo, because in his mind, the nigga was brainless and undisciplined. It didn't take a mind reader to see that Bolo's only dream was to make a quick dollar. "I'll tell you what. I got to handle some business downstairs in the basement. Help me discipline one of my churchgoers, and I'll front you a kilo of *manteca,* fifty-fifty me and you only. Fat Angel don't have to know about our side deal."

"Shit, who I got to smoke?"

"Nah, no killing, just a little discipline."

"Let's have it. I'm ready." Bolo was willing to do whatever it took to earn Flip Kilos's trust. He finally had a solid connection. *Thank you, Lord!*

Once in the basement, Bolo immediately recognized the target. Don Pepé from Hutchinson Street sat in a chair, bound and gagged.

"You see this old scumbag? He likes to touch little girls. He was busted touching a little girl from our Sunday school class. Because I'm such a nice person, I'm not gonna turn him in to the police. No, I'm going to serve him justice!" Flip said.

Flip untied the old man and yanked his pants down. Don Pepé stood there with his pants around his ankles. "Now bend this motherfucker over, and show him how it feels to get fucked," Flip Kilos said.

"What?"

"You heard me. Shove your big dick deep in this pervert's asshole."

"You trippin'," Bolo said.

"You want this product? Then do it. Teach this scumbag a lesson. Show him how it feels to be violated like the little girls he violates."

Don Pepé shook uncontrollably. Flip stuffed the handkerchief deeper into Don Pepé's mouth. The old man stared at him, fear evident in his eyes.

"Yo, that's asking too much," Bolo protested.

"Then we don't have a deal."

Bolo was wringing his hands. Flip Kilos pulled the heroin out to show Bolo again. "Do it and this is yours."

Bolo shook his head and unzipped his pants. He bent the old man over the chair and rammed his dick deep inside his asshole. Don Pepé's screams were muffled by the handkerchief. Flip Kilos was getting hard watching Bolo slam in and out. Bolo would never admit it, but it felt good, and he was enjoying the old man's tight asshole. He understood why niggas in jail were buttfucking each other.

Flip Kilos was rubbing his dick as he watched the two men go at it. He secretly wished he were the one Bolo was pounding. As soon as Bolo shot his load inside Don Pepé, Flip Kilos released his load all over the floor.

Flip and Bolo looked at each other. Flip nodded his head, and Bolo pulled his pants up. This secret would never leave the room.

"Yo, go get that pan of hot grease." Flip motioned to the pan of grease simmering on the stove.

Don Pepé shook his head frantically as sweat poured down his wrinkled face. Bolo was enjoying himself.

"Awful as it may seem, I'm cutting you some slack," Flip Kilos said to the old man as Bolo poured the hot grease over Don Pepé's naked groin.

The smell of burning flesh excited Bolo. The old man closed his eyes, screamed mercilessly, and passed out.

Flip and Bolo laughed. The fact was, Don Pepé had never bothered or touched any little girl. His only crime was being the grandfather of North Philly's most notorious killer, Lil' Bert. Flip had done his homework and singlehandedly picked out Don Pepé as a way of declaring war on Lil' Bert and his crew.

Fat Angel had shared the drama Bolo and Bert were having with Flip Kilos, and Flip decided to declare war on Bert with his new flunky in the frontline. Bolo was ready to swim in blood. On the other hand, Reverend Cruz was just a wannabe ex-drug dealer who didn't want to get his hands dirty.

"I want the old man to live, because I want to enjoy the pleasure of killing his grandson and anyone who might catch feelings about us disciplining this old child molester," Flip Kilos said, studying Bolo's face.

"Fuck him! He got what he deserved. He's lucky we just greased him up a little. By the way, who the fuck is his grandson?"

"Oh, you don't know? That old motherfucker's Lil' Bert's grandfather," Flip said, turning his back to the door leading to his office.

"I really don't care if that's his grandfather. In due time, I personally will deal with Bert myself. He owes me one anyway." Bolo was more concerned with having Flip Kilos front him a brick of *manteca* than he was about his own life.

After dumping Don Pepé on the corner of Glenwood Avenue, Flip Kilos and Bolo headed back to Flip's office, where Flip broke a key of *manteca* into quarters, cutting it up with Fentanyl and preparing it for distribution. "Believe me, young buck. Fiends will come to this dope like flies on shit. It's the best shit in town!"

"Yeah, I feel you on that!"

"It's almost time to claim our places in the history books of the drug game." Flip was putting Bolo on the dope-game ho strip and pimping him like a natural whore.

As he knew it would, the *manteca* he and Bolo put out on the streets had addicts selling their asses for a hit. It became a twenty-four-hour-a-day problem for the coroner's office in the City of Brotherly Love. Dozens of deaths occurred almost daily. For every addict who overdosed, twenty more flooded Second and Diamond Streets looking for Homicide, the street name for Flip and Bolo's heroin. Fiends longed for a bigger bang for their buck, and Flip was more than willing to help them turn their heroin and syringes into loaded guns.

Kensington was pegged as their principal distribution point in Philadelphia. Flip and Bolo were living large.

"We finally made it!" Bolo said as he sat at a table, counting money.

"Nah, not yet. We'll be on top when we're the only cats out here. Little by little, we're cornering the market. Man, I love it! We're doing what we're supposed to be doing. We're shaping the future. We're shaping history," Flip Kilos said as he stacked the $100 bills one on top of the other.

"Old head, this ain't the History Channel. These streets are real. My future is now. Fuck tomorrow! I live for today!"

"Damn, youngster! You need to slow down! Think before you act! Money's always gonna be on the streets. The hardest part of this game is staying alive. Everybody wants to go after the man, and right now, you are the man of the hour."

"I guess Biggie said it best: 'You ain't nobody 'til somebody kills you.'"

"Hopefully you'll get to enjoy some of this cash, youngster."

"You ain't never lied, old head!" Bolo said, and then added, "When I go, I want to go out like Scarface with a machine gun blazing."

"Now that's how the big boys are supposed to play! Hustle with real hustlers, little nigga!" Flip said, giving Bolo a pound before he walked out of the basement.

Chapter Fifteen

An Eye for an Eye

For reasons nobody understood, Detective Ruiz had an intense dislike for Lil' Bert. Detectives usually disliked criminals, but this hate was more like an obsession. In his opinion, Bert was responsible for a number of high-profile murders in the city, and the detective was making a career out of pursuing him. Though he tried to mask his frustration, Detective Ruiz's ego was deflated when he couldn't get witnesses to drop a dime on Bert.

Ruiz sat in front of Papo's Beer Distributors, studying Franklin Street and wondering how a rough and decaying section of the city could generate so much illegal income. He thought of Papo, his new source of information, and waited until the beer shop was empty before he paid him a visit. He didn't have the patience or the stomach for the unmistakable smell of death emanating from the Franklin Street neighborhood.

When Papo spotted Detective Ruiz walking through the glass door, he knew what the dick was coming for. Papo was old school, straightforward, and wasn't about to cut corners with Detective Ruiz. He was determined to remain free at all costs, and that was why he warped the code of the streets to fit his own needs. Deep down in his heart, Papo knew he was caught up in the twisted cycle of codependence with Detective Ruiz.

"What's goin' on, amigo?" Detective Ruiz extended his hand to Papo in a friendly manner.

"Everything's cool," Papo responded.

"Are you sure?"

"Yeah. If it weren't, you'd be the first to hear about it. Why do you ask?"

"No particular reason. I'm just concerned, that's all."

"Should I be worried about anything?"

"Always," Detective Ruiz said.

"To what do I owe this honor?" Papo asked. Beads of sweat started to form on his nose.

"I just want to catch up on the rumors the streets are carrying. You know, about Lil' Bert and his partner not being a tag team anymore," Detective Ruiz said, removing his cigarettes from his pocket.

"The only thing I know is that Lil' Bert has a new, young nigga by the name of Black Manny who's running the streets, claiming to be the shot caller."

"Really?"

"Yeah."

"Where did this so-called Black Manny pop up from?" Detective Ruiz asked.

"The only thing I know is that he just came home from doing a five-year bid, and he's already putting niggas out of business. I'm telling you, this kid is trigger-happy! He shot a dude in a Chinese store two days ago just because the dude jumped in front of him in line. After he shot the dude, he spit in the Chinese lady's face who served the dude."

"Why in the hell would someone do some shit like that? Especially if they're fresh out of jail!" Detective Ruiz exclaimed.

"My point is that you just can't pop up in here at any time of the day you want. I don't want to end up with a bullet in my head because of you. That's not what floats my boat."

"So why did you decide to become my snitch?"

"That's cruel!"

"Asshole, don't get sentimental on me! I cut you a break by not booking you on a charge of murder one. It's never too late to do it either."

"I was just trying to make a difference."

"Bullshit! You were trying to save your ass!"

"Nah, Detective, I was doing my civic duty!" Papo insisted.

"Listen to me carefully. I don't give a shit about you, your feelings, or anyone else on this dumpy ghetto block. I want Lil' Bert and whoever runs with him put away for life, and you're going to help me put him there, because if you don't, I swear to you, I will pin every unsolved murder in North Philly on you, trust me! I have the powers backing me on this, *pendejo!*"

Papo was uncomfortable but remained quiet for a few seconds. "Man, who's gonna protect my babies and me when this crazy-ass nigga comes after me? I'm not trying to make my kids orphans."

"Collateral damage, Papo!"

"Aw, hell no! I'll have your mothafucking badge for this! I ain't scared of you! I'll—" Papo stopped in midsentence when he heard the screeching tires of a dark blue Lexus that pulled up in front of the beer shop.

The driver got out of the car and walked into the beer shop. He ordered a case of orange juice and glanced around while he waited. He was a dark-skinned man in his mid-twenties with long, wavy hair. His birth name was Manny Sanchez, but the streets and state prisons across Pennsylvania called this five foot ten inch man "Black Manny" or "Hands of Death." He was wearing several diamonds in his ears, on his wrists, and around his neck. He was iced out.

Detective Ruiz stared in Black Manny's direction. Something about the man made him feel uneasy.

"S'up, old-timer? What do I owe you?" Manny asked Papo after he placed the case of juice on the counter.

"Twenty-one dollars," Papo said.

Manny peeled off a $100 bill from a thick wad of bills and placed it on top of the counter. Then he snatched up the case of orange juice and headed for the door.

"Sir! Sir!" Papo shouted, waving his hands in the air. "You forgot your change!"

"Nah, I ain't forget. Give it to that fat mothafucka who's mean mugging me there," Black Manny said, making eye contact with Detective Ruiz while exposing the butt of his 9 mm in his belt.

"Whoa, whoa, whoa! It ain't that serious, young buck!" Papo said.

"A'ight, then!"

"I just want to give you your change."

"What'd I say? Give it to your friend there," Black Manny said.

Detective Ruiz felt hatred in the room. In his twenty-seven years as a detective, he'd never felt fear in the course of doing his duty as a cop. Now he found himself standing in front of his snitch, doubting his ability to serve and protect the citizens of the City of Brotherly Love. *Maybe I'm getting too old for this.*

"So that's the new boss in town, huh?" Detective Ruiz asked after Black Manny left.

"Yeah, fresh out of the joint."

"Keep me informed," the detective said. He walked out in a hurry and sped off in his unmarked car.

For the next two months, Detective Ruiz dedicated all his time to gathering information on Lil' Bert and Black Manny. Early one morning, he received a call that changed the course of his investigation. As the sun broke through the city, the body of a Hispanic male was discovered hanging from a stop sign pole at the corner of Franklin and Indiana Avenue. Two words, STOP SNITCH-ING, were spray-painted on the stop sign itself. When Detective Ruiz arrived on the scene, he was shocked to see that the man hanging from the pole was none other than Papo.

As the other homicide detectives secured the crime scene, Detective Ruiz searched Papo's pockets, and it took a few minutes for him to identify what he had found in the shirt pocket. His brain worked hard to find the right words to identify the object he was holding in his hand. His knees buckled and his stomach lurched wildly. Detective Ruiz was holding Papo's rotten tongue in the palm of his hand. He fell to his knees and vomited on the street corner.

"Hey, it's okay, Ruiz. Take it easy, man. Sit back, partner. I got this," his partner said.

Ruiz waved off the rookie cop and sat up slowly, his head reeling. "I'm okay."

"You sure? You hit the ground pretty hard," the rookie cop said.

"I'm fine, really."

He'd never passed out in his life, not even back when he'd gotten the news that his daughter was dead. It wasn't just Papo's tongue. He'd seen worse before. It was something else that had struck him like a bullet and made him lose his breakfast. It was as if Papo's tongue had established a conduit between himself and the savage who had killed Papo. For an instant, a door swung open in his mind, and Detective Ruiz peered inside the devious mind of the street savage who killed Papo. The utter blackness sucked at him, tugged and struggled to pull him in. Had he not passed out, he would have had a massive heart attack.

Chapter Sixteen

Feel the Pain

Black Manny and Lil' Bert listened to the intense moans and groans of sex as they crept into Reverend Cruz's house. They knew instantly that some serious fucking was going on, and they both swelled with excitement. Someone was getting her pussy pounded and her freak on at the same time.

"Oh, my Gawd! Ohh! Ughh! Ughh!"

"Woooo! Woooo! Woooo! Ahhhh!"

Lil' Bert and Black Manny stood outside Reverend Cruz's bedroom door, and the voice that only seconds ago sounded like a female's now had a deeper tone, sounding more like a young boy getting reamed in the shower of a penitentiary. Lil' Bert and Black Manny both looked at each other in disgust.

In the pit of his stomach, Lil' Bert felt a strange sensation. He was riddled with guilt for allowing his grandpop to get caught up in his street business. The streets were deadlier than ever for him. "Somebody's gotta die!" he mumbled as he kicked Reverend Cruz's bedroom door open.

"What da fuck?" Bolo hollered. He was balls-deep in Reverend Cruz's bent-over asshole.

"Bitch-ass nigga! If you move, I will blow your wig back! Test me if you want!" Black Manny said, wanting to get this shit over with quickly.

But Bert had other plans for Bolo. "Both of you faggot mothafuckas, lie down on the bed face-first!" he ordered.

"Can I at least put some goddamn clothes on, nigga?" Bolo pleaded as he tried to get up off the bed.

"Nigga, what part of 'don't get up' you don't understand?" Black Manny said, smacking Bolo in his head with his gun.

Bolo remained conscious, but his head was split wide open. The reality of his plight was sinking in. Although he tried to talk tough, he knew if he was to buy any time to save his life, he had better start following Lil' Bert's orders. So he lay his sweaty, naked body on the bed face-first.

Black Manny pulled out a roll of duct tape and covered Reverend Cruz's mouth. Bert unzipped a bag full of goodies he had brought along for the mission.

"Nigga, if y'all gonna kill me, do it! I'm ready to die!" Bolo hollered and spit toward Bert's direction.

"You faggot-ass bitch! I'ma teach you some fucking manners!" Bert said, smiling maliciously as he took his gun and pounded Bolo in the mouth until pieces of his gold grill exploded out of his mouth. "Duct-tape that bitch up, Black!" Bert was laughing at the pathetic pleas Bolo was making through a mouth that was duct-taped shut.

"Listen, we can make this simple. Y'all speak only when spoken to. I'ma remove the tape from your mouth, and if you speak out of order, I will kill you!" Bert said, then added, "Black, sit those two bitch-ass faggots up. Now where are the drugs and money?" he asked, looking directly at Reverend Cruz.

"Are you going to kill me?"

"It's up to you, faggot. I can easily put a bullet between your eyes. It depends if you're gonna waste my time or if you're gonna answer my questions truthfully."

Reverend Cruz saw his whole life flash in front of him. At that moment, he had second thoughts about bullshitting the two killers in front of him. Robbery registered in Reverend Cruz's mind, and he thought, *this doesn't have to turn into a homicide.* Then he started spilling his guts to the two killers. "Man, there's close to two hundred thousand dollars, cash, in my safe, four bricks of coke, and three bricks of heroin. The combination is three rotations right, stop on twenty-five. Then two full rotations left, stop at two. Then one full rotation back to the right and stop on sixteen. Take it all. Just don't kill me!" he pleaded to Bert.

Bert shoved Bolo's underwear in Reverend Cruz's mouth, duct-taped his mouth shut, and told Black Manny to kill both of them if they so much as blinked.

Bert opened the door to Cruz's walk-in closet and opened the safe. There was $200,000 in cash, a stack of videotapes, cassette tapes, four handguns, a pile of jewelry, and all the drugs the reverend promised. As he stepped out of the closet, he flipped on the plasma TV and inserted one of the tapes he found into the DVD player. He reasoned that if they were hiding in the safe, they must contain something real hot that the good reverend didn't want anyone else to view.

Bert scanned the video. Most of the footage contained scenes of Reverend Cruz getting his back twisted in what seemed like consensual sex with all types of homosexual thugs. The video soon gave way to more disturbing images of Reverend Cruz passionately kissing on a young girl. Whoever the girl was, her face had been blotted out of the video.

As Bert continued to fast forward the tape, he saw Reverend Cruz pushing the girl toward the mahogany desk, sitting her down gently, then separating her legs and sliding her little panties to the side and massaging her little pink clit with his fingers. His kneading and probing had the girl rocking to the rhythm of his strokes. Just when he was about to slide his dick in the girl, she pushed away and dropped to her knees and revealed her identity.

Bert's anger took control of his body as he stared at Reverend Cruz with bloodshot eyes, pointing his 9 mm directly at his head. "Punk bitch! I should kill you right now, but I'm not! I want you to answer my questions! Who is the girl in the video? If you have to think about the answer, I'll kill you!"

"She's just a trick I play with from time to time. She's nobody important," Reverend Cruz responded, looking confused.

"What's her name?"

"MaryLuz. I only know her first name." Rev. Cruz was now quivering, and his voice gave out on him. He lost control of his bowels.

"Nigga! This punk-ass bitch just shit on himself, man! Just kill these motherfuckas, and let's get the fuck out of here!" Black Manny tried not to breathe in the smell of shit and Bolo's cum that was mixed in it.

"Nah, be easy, kid. I want to torture both of these niggas. See, these niggas here are responsible for my grandfather having the heart attack he just had. They're the ones who poured hot grease on him, so now they must suffer the same pain," Bert said, striking a chord in Black Manny.

Bert then turned his attention to Bolo, satisfied that Black Manny was not going to interfere or hurry him one way or the other. "Nigga, you must be crazy if you didn't think I was gonna get at you for what you did to my people."

Bolo didn't even flinch, thrusting out his chest, trying to look hard.

Bert was impressed. He was used to killing chumps like Bolo. "Did you hear what I said?" he asked him.

"Fuck you, nigga! It is what it is! Now do you! You're nothing, man! Look at you! I fucked your grandfather up, and all you do is stand there and ask me why!" Bolo yelled, his eyes burning with rage and frustration.

"The stakes are high. You will pay the price with your life."

"What would your grandpa think of you, huh? How would he feel to know that his grandson is too much of a pussy to take out the guy who tortured him and is now talking shit to his supposed killa grandson?" Bolo was pulling all the tricks out of the bag, trying to buy some time on his life.

It was useless. The swell of anger Bert was feeling since breaking through Reverend Cruz's bedroom door just wouldn't go away. Shooting Bolo to death was an easy task, but he wanted to inflict lots of pain on the motherfucker. He wanted Bolo to feel the pain he felt when he finally came around to shooting him. Bolo had to die. Bert's reputation was all he had. Without it, he was nothing.

Bert looked at Black Manny and instructed him to duct-tape Bolo's mouth shut. Afterward, he gripped Bolo by the neck, bent him over the bed, and pulled out a curling iron from the bag he'd brought with him. He plugged it in and worked the long iron up inside Bolo's black ass.

The muffled agony Bolo released only made Bert angrier. "Talk dat shit now, mothafucka!" Bert kept pushing the curling iron into Bolo's ass until his body jerked and blood poured out of his asshole.

"Black, bring both of these punks into the bathroom!"

Black did as he was instructed while Bert gripped Bolo by the hair and dragged him into the bathroom.

"Kneel down!" Black barked at Reverend Cruz.

Bert ran back into the bedroom and grabbed a pillow, returned to the bathroom, and closed the door behind him. "Yo, Black, put dat nigga's head in the toilet bowl," Bert said, pointing at Bolo. Bert then placed the pillow over Bolo's head and shoved the gun into the pillow, pulling the trigger without hesitation. Chunks of Bolo's skull and brain floated in the toilet bowl. His motionless body went limp on the cold bathroom floor. Like the coldhearted killer he was, Bert removed a knife from his pocket, leaned down, and cut Bolo's dick off.

Reverend Cruz knew that he himself was done too, as Black Manny put a bullet in his brain.

Bert stuffed Bolo's dick in Reverend Cruz's mouth and duct-taped it shut again.

Chapter Seventeen

No Love 4 a Gangster

The news of Bolo's and Reverend Cruz's deaths traveled quickly through the streets of Philly. Niggas who were supposed to be on Bolo's team were now looking to exploit the situation by robbing Bolo's stash house. Others were trying to find new alliances with the next nigga on the come-up. Jay was no exception. He knew this was the time to make his move to solidify his position in the drug game in Philly.

"I can't believe my nigga is dead! I told him to be careful with dat preacher boy!" Jay blared out as he lit a blunt.

"Word on the block is them two clowns were fucking, blowing each other's back out," Pito joked. He showed no remorse for his slain friend.

In truth, Jay was happy to finally have the opportunity to shine on his own. He felt he should inherit Bolo's position because he was his right-hand man. At that moment, he raised his blunt, declaring himself the new boss. "To a new start at life! *Salud!*" he said.

Pito toasted up his own blunt.

Jay was now the nigga he'd been itching to be, but he lacked the heart it took to be the boss.

Bolo's body was laid out in Rodriguez's Funeral Parlor in North Philly, located at Fifth and Cayuga. It looked more like a Jay-Z concert than a funeral of a wannabe drug dealer. Bolo was a chump—a rat faggot who fucked his way into the elite of the drug game. No one was particularly sad he was dead.

The gold diggers of the community showed up in packs. Fat asses shook from chickenheads who mingled with hustlers as if they were in a nightclub. It felt more like a celebration than mourning. The people were there to be seen and to hook up.

Bert and his crew sat in the back row and listened to the rumors about who murdered Bolo and Reverend Cruz. The guessing game was in full effect. MS-13 were the prime suspects, which brought happiness to Bert, because that meant that no one would be looking his way.

Some of Bolo's loyalists whispered among themselves about Bert's attendance, but none of them had the heart to step to him.

"Damn, big homie! When you come home?" Jay asked as he walked up to Bert and Black Manny.

"I've been home for a minute," Black Manny responded.

"The least you could do is give a nigga a hug. Ain't nothing changed. I'm the same nigga who grew up with you. I'm happy to see you," Jay said as he reached into his pocket, pulled out a roll of bills, and handed them over to Black Manny.

"I'm safe, homie. I'm not here for no handout. I'm here to pay respects to our friend."

"My bad! I meant no disrespect. I just thought I'd look out for a friend who just did a long bid," Jay said, putting the roll of bills back into his pocket.

"None taken," Black Manny replied.

"Damn, dawg! It's fucked up how they did your people. I'd hate to be the nigga who did it," Bert said, turning to face Jay. He wanted to see where he stood.

"Yeah. Niggas gonna bleed over this. Believe that, big homie. I'm gonna rep his legacy 'til I die."

"Nigga, who you think you talking to? I see the bitch in your eyes! You the man now, right? Fuck you care about that faggot-bitch nigga who got his brains blown the fuck out in a toilet?" Bert asked, looking Jay dead in the eyes.

"You getting beside yourself, disrespecting my man up in his funeral! Watch yo' damn mouth!" Pito said, fronting like he was a killer or like he gave a fuck.

"Jay, you could stand here and act like you don't know who I am and let that fake-ass nigga run his mouth and get killed. Or you could man up and play your part. Either way, which one of you niggas is going to inherit the beef Bolo and I have?" Bert knew he had Jay shook.

Jay stared at Bert in a state of confusion. *What now?* he asked himself as he quickly searched for a comeback line. Not responding to Bert would make him look like a cold-blooded pussy. "Nah, that beef is dead. Squashed. Bolo's beef with you was between y'all. I got nothing to do with that." Jay felt intimidated, but he couldn't show it.

"You wrong. My beef was and still is with all you punk mothafuckas! Don't bitch up because y'all's leader is dead!"

By now a crowd of onlookers was standing around ear hustling, trying to see if any drama was about to kick off.

"Man, let's go somewhere private and discuss this," Jay suggested. Lil' Bert's name planted fear in niggas' hearts in Philly. If the streets saw Jay and Lil' Bert together, they would think Jay's shit was official.

Lil' Bert read right through his bitch ass and saw his intention. "Nah, it ain't that kind of party, playboy. So what's it gonna be?" He didn't wait for a reply. He was a veteran at this shit. He started walking out of the funeral home, leaving Jay standing in front of his new crew looking like a complete nut.

"I don't want no beef with you," Jay said as he walked behind Lil' Bert and his crew.

Lil' Bert and Black Manny slid in the back seat of a dark blue Lexus, smiling to themselves as they watched Jay shake in fear.

Shyla was looking as good as ever. It had been four months since she'd entered rehab, and she was starting to see the benefits. She was gaining her weight back, her ass was shaping up, and she no longer looked like a crack whore. She vowed to never let another nigga pimp her out or beat her down. From now on, niggas would only have two options: lace her up or keep moving. She was determined to go hard on the streets.

After all Bolo put her through, it was a no-brainer when Lil' Bert approached her with a proposition to set Bolo up. Since the day Bolo had beaten her ass like a runaway slave, she'd stopped riding with him.

One night she had been walking back to the women's shelter on Thirteenth and Erie after her daily NA meeting, and she was feeling good until she suddenly came face-to-face with Lil' Bert. "Oh, shit!" she blurted out when she saw his nine aiming at her head. *I don't wanna die!*

"I'll kill you if I have to," she heard the restrained voice say. "If you work with me, then you can live. You decide what you want to do."

"What can I help you with?" Shyla sounded confident.

"All I want to know is where Bolo is resting his head at night. If you bullshit me, I'll take your life."

"I don't mess with him anymore."

"Bitch, don't test me! Technically, you don't have nothing to do with this, but you'll die right here if you fuck with me."

"So if I give you the address where Bolo stays, you'll let me walk away?"

"My word is my bond."

It was a joy for Shyla to blurt out, "2107 Howard Street. And when you do catch up with that mothafucka, tell him to eat shit and die!"

Bert reached inside his pants pocket and pulled out a wad of cash and started counting out loud. When he reached $5,000, he handed Shyla the money. "This conversation never took place, you hear me?" He then walked away, never looking back at her.

Shyla gripped the money and smiled. She never shed a tear or felt any guilt about Bolo's death. As far as she was concerned, he'd gotten what he deserved. "Rest in peace, you sheisty-ass nigga!" she said as she tucked the five Gs in her jeans pocket and continued down the street.

Chapter Eighteen

Da Streets Are Talking

MaryLuz knew the streets were buzzing with her name. Rumor had it that she was the hottest thing on video since Paris Hilton.

"Girl, I'm telling you, niggas on the block are copping your tape like it's dope!" Tete said, shaking her neck from side to side.

MaryLuz gasped in shock, not wanting to believe what she was hearing. *This has to be a mistake.* Her mind was playing tricks on her. In a matter of seconds, she went over every trick she'd ever been with in the last six months, and still she came up with nothing. She wasn't sloppy with her shit. *This can't be me. It's probably some look-alike ho who stole my style.* She felt somewhat better, but women's intuition was telling her something else. "Tete, you need to get one of those tapes for me, 'cause I don't recall getting dirty in front of no camera. I don't do the R. Kelly thing. Nevertheless, I want to see it for myself."

Tete was giving MaryLuz a scandalous stare. "Bitch, cut it the fuck out! It's you on that tape."

"Nah, it can't be. I don't get down like that." Tears trickled down MaryLuz's face.

"Okay, if you say so, but I don't know if I can get my hands on one of those tapes. But I'm saying, I saw the tape last night, and it's you, baby girl. The nigga I'm messing with popped it in while he was beating my pussy up," Tete said. She checked her cell phone for messages.

"Who the fuck is dis nigga anyway?" MaryLuz asked, almost whispering.

"They call him Black Manny, and he's fine as hell. Got a good head game, knows how to keep the pussy popping and snapping, and believe me, girl, he's packing at least twelve inches, so yes! I'm deep throating him every chance I get! This nigga is already open on this pussy. In fact, we're going shopping tomorrow. You know how I do," Tete said as she rubbed her pussy through her jeans.

"Bitch, do you! But get a copy of that tape," MaryLuz said as she walked into her bathroom, slamming the door behind her.

"Don't be mad at me 'cause you got caught, stinking whore!" Tete yelled, smiling to herself. *Fuck that whore! She thinks she's all that anyway. I hope every nigga on the block gets a copy of her fucking on tape. That's what she gets for trying to be slick. Bitch be tricking on the down low. Fuck her!*

Tete had resentment for MaryLuz for not hooking her up with a job at police headquarters, and she wasn't the type to keep a secret. Although the girls she hung out with and grew up with appreciated her friendship, none would share with her the dirt they did on the side. If they did, they knew Tete would air them out like *The Wendy Williams Show*. Tete had loose lips.

MaryLuz had recommended Felicia, another professional dick sucker from around the way, for the job, and Tete felt MaryLuz was the reason she had to go on welfare. While Felicia and MaryLuz were stacking paper and going on shopping sprees, Tete had to settle for a monthly check from Uncle Sam and suck on a few dicks on the side for extra money. *Fuck that bitch! Payback is a mothafucka!*

MaryLuz came out of the bathroom several minutes later, feeling estranged and betrayed. A hole gnawed in her stomach that demanded to be filled. She turned toward Tete and said in an irritated voice, "I'm hungry as hell. What about you?"

"Yeah. What'cha cooking?" Tete responded as she followed MaryLuz into the kitchen.

"Chicken and mac and cheese."

"Sounds good to me," Tete said as she dipped her hand into a mound of grapes and popped several into her mouth one at a time. She watched MaryLuz's tears gather at the corner of her eye. Yes, indeed, she felt like a liberated woman. She sanctioned all the emotional bullshit MaryLuz was feeling. *Suffer the consequences, bitch! I hate you!* "Why you stressing the small things in life? I told you I got you. Plus, if you say you ain't do it, then I believe you. So chill!" she said, giving MaryLuz a concerned look.

Damn, I'm slipping! Just a few days ago I was the baddest bitch on the block, on point, scheming on all the trick niggas trying to get in my panties. Yeah, I was the center of attention. Now I'm stressing and tripping about some dumb shit. Hell, I need a drink. MaryLuz poured herself a drink from a bottle of vodka sitting on top of her kitchen counter.

Tete, being the dirty bitch she was, decided to add venom to the drama in MaryLuz's life. "You know, sometimes these niggas out here make me sick! Don't get me wrong, I'm strictly dickly, but no nigga can give me the understanding and compassion a bitch can." She put emphasis on the words "bitch can."

MaryLuz's ass was peeking out beneath the long T-shirt she sported, which drove Tete crazy with desire. Although she claimed not to be a dyke, she enjoyed and welcomed the opportunity to have the walls of her pussy licked and eaten out. She had experienced her first lesbian affair six months ago while spending the night at MaryLuz's. Although they'd both blamed it on the alcohol they'd consumed, Tete knew MaryLuz was turned out on some side pussy. In fact, she'd been creeping on the down low with a black chick from South Philly who was supposed to be a prison guard at Graterford Prison.

"I'm horny as hell!" Tete blared out as she swayed close to MaryLuz.

"I'm horny too, but—"

Tete spun MaryLuz around and began grinding into her fat ass and moved her hand to her crotch, popping two fingers into her juicy, wet pussy and toying with her clit. MaryLuz moaned and rocked her hips back and forth against Tete's hands.

"Hold up!" Tete said, withdrawing her hand from MaryLuz's pussy and then licking her fingers. She disappeared into the living room, and when she returned seconds later, she had a seductive smile on her face that was more intoxicating than the Ecstasy pill she was about to place into MaryLuz's mouth. "Here!" Tete said, nibbling on her bottom lip while letting her hand roam along MaryLuz's hard nipples.

When Tete slid her fingers back into her pussy, she discovered that MaryLuz had removed her panties. Tete was burning with fire and desire. Her panties were soaked and hot at the crotch. "Let me take my jeans off," she whispered, kissing MaryLuz on the back of the neck.

"I want to eat your panties off you, so leave them on," MaryLuz said. She removed her T-shirt and stood in front of Tete stark naked, her pussy dripping and her nipples as hard as bullets.

Tete wasted no time laying MaryLuz on top of the kitchen table and spreading her legs. She licked her pussy and asshole, and when she was finished drinking MaryLuz's juices, she inserted an E in her asshole.

MaryLuz was lost in a world she never knew existed. She came over and over again, and on her sixth orgasm, she fainted.

Being the hateful bitch Tete was, she pulled out her cell phone and recorded MaryLuz getting her lesbian freak on. Before she was finished, she slid the neck of the vodka bottle up MaryLuz's ass.

When MaryLuz awakened the following day, Tete was long gone. As sore as her pussy was, she knew the night before had been nothing but lovely. *Damn, I don't even remember how I ended up in the bedroom!* When she looked at her watch, it was one o'clock in the afternoon. She reached for her cell phone and dialed her work number. When the receptionist answered, she feigned sickness.

Usually, MaryLuz would be at work planning out her next trick, but today she was home lying in a hot bath, recovering from the delicious shit she'd been a part of the night before. She shrugged her shoulders and closed her eyes, satisfied that her pussy was aching and wanting more.

Chapter Nineteen

Old News

The next day, MaryLuz tried to reach Tete, but every time she called, she got her voice mail. She paced back and forth in her office until five o'clock came around. Then she stormed out of police headquarters and headed for North Philly in search of Tete. She searched all the places she thought Tete would be but came up empty. After three hours of searching, she went home. It was beyond her nature to be longing for anyone, let alone a lesbo dyke. Here she was, nervous, upset, tripping, and wondering why Tete hadn't called her. *Why hasn't she called? Why didn't she wake me up before she bounced? Why doesn't she answer her phone? Fuck it. It's her loss!* She fell asleep, confident that Tete would holler at her soon.

Hours later, MaryLuz woke up and immediately checked her voicemail. There was no message from Tete. Against her better judgment, she gave Lil' Bert a call.

"Hello?"

"What's up, *papi?*"

"S'up?" Bert said in a cold tone.

"I miss you."

"Whatever!" Bert snapped. "Why you calling me?"

"What do you mean, why am I calling you? I told you I miss you!"

"Bitch, we got nothing to talk about, so lose my number, video whore!"

Click!

MaryLuz stared at her cell phone in disbelief. "I know this stupid-ass nigga didn't just hang up on me!" she said, putting her cell phone down on the table.

Days turned into weeks, and there was still no word from Tete. Eventually, MaryLuz decided that she'd been played. Then one day, she spotted Tete leaning against the building of the Spanish cuchifrito restaurant at Fifth and Lehigh and talking to a dark-skinned Puerto Rican. MaryLuz had been on her way to visit her mother, but she quickly slammed on the brakes and double-parked. She walked quickly toward Tete. "Tete!" she called out. She was hoping for some kind of explanation.

"What's going on, MaryLuz?"

"What's going on? Why the fuck haven't you called me?"

"For what? I got a life to live," Tete said bluntly.

Black Manny stared at MaryLuz with lust in his eyes and a vicious hard-on. "Yo, you the chick from the video! Damn! You sure got a fat ass! Yo, why don't you let me hit that?" Black Manny said, bursting out laughing.

"Fuck you, nigga!"

"Nah, baby, fuck you! That's what I wanna do to you. Fuck you in the ass. Believe me, it'll be better than a bottle!" Black Manny said, pulling out his cell phone. He flipped it open and revealed the footage of Tete molesting MaryLuz's brown eye.

MaryLuz stood there, her jaw dropping in disbelief.

"If you need a manager, holler at your boy!"

MaryLuz turned around to see who the voice belonged to, and to her surprise, Lil' Bert was standing there smirking from ear to ear.

"You dirty bitch!" MaryLuz yelled at Tete. "I thought you were my friend! How could you do this to me?"

"Friend! Bitch, you thought wrong! I ain't got no friends! You were just a shot of ass, a good pussy to lick and flip. Other than that, you're old news. It is what it is, whore!" Tete said, pointing her finger in MaryLuz's face.

"I'ma beat your ass right here, right now!" MaryLuz said, punching Tete in the face. But before MaryLuz could grab a handful of Tete's hair, Lil' Bert pimp slapped her and split her lip wide open. "Bitch, step before you get hurt!" he said, feeling his own rage boiling inside of him.

"*Cabron!* You're gonna pay for this!"

Lil' Bert smiled impishly, enjoying the emotional breakdown MaryLuz was experiencing. Disrespecting her was almost as good as getting a nut to him. *The bitch played herself. I should beat her ass out here in front of the whole block.* "Bitch, I said bounce before you get hurt!"

"Nigga, you're not gonna do shit! You little-dick moth-afucka! Fuck you and anybody who rolls with you! You're gonna pay for this, nigga!"

"Nah, you're gonna pay for this, you stupid bitch!" Lil' Bert said and punched MaryLuz dead in her face, knocking her out cold. He kicked her in the ribs several times as she lay sprawled out on the ground. "Don't ever disrespect me!" he said, kicking MaryLuz one last time in the side of her head.

She'd been played.

Chapter Twenty

Da Clock Is Ticking

The news of MaryLuz's beatdown traveled around North Philly like FedEx. Everybody who was anybody in the drug game began to distance themselves from her. Not because she had played herself by appearing in a sex video with a tricked-out homo, but because she worked in the homicide unit at police headquarters. No one wanted to be associated with the drama that was about to unfold. The stakes were high, and there was too much money out in the streets to be made for anyone to get caught up in any lovey-dovey scandal.

To Ito, none of that shit mattered. He wanted to strike back with deadly force. His favorite cousin had been violated in the worst way. Rumors were running in the streets about him as he wondered how that no-good nigga Lil' Bert, a nigga he had broken bread with, could do what he had done to his people.

As he sat in his aunt's house, he couldn't believe what he was hearing. "Are you sure Bert and Black Manny were the ones who beat MaryLuz down?" he asked his aunt Carmen.

"Maybe you should go out there and find out for yourself instead of sitting here like a fucking *mamao*. After all, they're your friends," his aunt said.

Without saying another word, Ito stormed out of the house. It was his reputation that was taking a hit. Even his aunt was calling him names.

It had been six months since he left the game alone, and for the entire time, the streets kept calling his name. He was no longer known as Lil' Bert's right-hand man. Ever since the rumors had begun that he was a confidential informer, his new handle was Loose Lips Ito. He was the hottest topic on every drug corner. He had been awarded the snitch label, and the green light was given to anyone who wanted to earn some stripes by introducing him to permanent darkness.

His people expected him to handle his business the only way he knew how, but he had other plans. The code of the streets had been broken a long time ago. That was one of the reasons he had left the game. *Why stop now? Fuck it! I'd rather be labeled a rat than a fly nigga in jail serving life.* He dialed his connect at police headquarters. "Hello, Detective Ruiz?"

"Yeah, it's me." Detective Ruiz recognized Ito's voice immediately. "I've been trying to reach you for over a week. Where the hell have you been?"

"Calm down or this conversation is over!" Ito said as arrogantly as he could.

"Listen to me, you piece of shit! You fucked up my operation by not contacting me like you were supposed to. We had a contract. If you want to play games, I'll book you with every case I have open. I put my ass on the line to keep you from going to prison. The clock is ticking, so now what are you going to do?"

"I'll deliver Lil' Bert and the rest of those assholes to you as promised. Have a little faith in my ability. Right now, I have some family matters I must attend to. I give you my word I'll see you in two days." Ito was trying to convince Detective Ruiz that he had something worth waiting for.

"Okay, okay! What do you have that's worth waiting for? I need something so my supervisor doesn't pull the plug."

"Tell your supervisor I'll wear a wire and I'll talk to the DA."

"Okay, but if you don't produce, they're going to charge you with two counts of first-degree murder. It's the DA's call. You're looking at the death penalty for the murder of Lucy Mendez and her unborn child," Detective Ruiz said with a smile.

"Like I said, I have some family matters to attend to. I'll come see you in two days," Ito replied and turned his cell phone off before Detective Ruiz could say another word.

"Lieutenant, I just finished talking to my informant, and he has agreed to wear a wire. He'll be in to see me in person in forty-eight hours. I think we may have our big break."

"That's about enough, Ruiz! Your rat's been MIA for a while, and now he's calling you and dictating how we do things? No! That's not how it works. If he doesn't give us information that we can use to bring down the Suicidal Riders, he's gonna be charged with those murders!" Lieutenant Smith said as he pounded on his desk with his fist.

"Lieutenant, he's going to come through. Have I ever let you down?"

"That's not the point! I'm getting political pressure from the top, Ruiz! We need shit that's going to send this Lil' Bert asshole to his death. I don't want any circumstantial bullshit. I want solid evidence of multiple murders. Anything less will be unacceptable, understand me? Now get out of my office! I've got work of my own to do!"

**

Ito rushed past the security guard at the Temple University Hospital entrance and headed right for the receptionist's desk.

"Sorry, sir, visiting hours are over," the Puerto Rican receptionist said, giving Ito a look that made him smile.

Playing on her flirtatiousness, Ito leaned forward and whispered in her ear, "How about if I make this worth your while? I really need to see my sister. Afterward, we can enjoy a cup of coffee together," he said while sliding a $100 bill into her cleavage.

"Okay." She led him down the long corridor and into the room where MaryLuz was staying. Before she opened the door, she squeezed Ito's groin. "I can take care of this now!"

Her straightforwardness brought a smile to Ito's face. "I'll bet you can! But I'd rather wait until I see my sister." Ito had no intention of ever seeing the receptionist again.

The antiseptic smell of the hospital made Ito sick to his stomach. That smell represented illness and death, the two things Ito feared most. As he entered MaryLuz's room, anger took over his whole body.

MaryLuz turned her head toward the door as Ito walked into the room. She smiled, and even though she looked bad, she tried to put up a front.

"What did those niggas do to you?" Ito cried out in rage.

"Damn, bro! Do I look that bad?"

"Nah, you're still beautiful, baby girl."

He hounded MaryLuz for all the details of what had happened to her, and she could clearly see the dead seriousness in her cousin's eyes. "Chill, man! I'm all right. That bitch Tete set me up." MaryLuz never mentioned her lesbo affair with Tete, nor her appearance on the video, which had started this whole drama. She knew that sooner or later Ito would find out.

Ito stared at MaryLuz, his hands balled into two tight fists. "I told you to stay away from Bert! Didn't I tell you not to fuck with him?"

"I'm sorry!" MaryLuz whispered.

"Those niggas got to pay for this! He's gotta deal with me now!"

"Relax, Ito. You don't need to play yourself. I got plans of my own for that animal."

"Nah, it ain't that simple, baby girl. He disrespected you, knowing you're my people. You just stay here and get well. I'm out!"

He walked out of the room and past the receptionist nurse. "Are we still gonna enjoy that cup of coffee together?" she asked.

"Bitch, move before I slap the freak out of you!" he said, hurrying down the long hospital corridor.

Chapter Twenty-one

Two for One

It was another blazing hot August day, one of the hottest ever recorded. News stations around the city were warning people to stay inside. Indoor recreational centers and air-conditioned churches were open to anyone looking to cool off.

For Black Manny and Three Finger June, this was the day they would kill Ito. They'd been following him for days, tracking his every move and not believing what they were witnessing. Ito had pulled his 600 SE into the parking lot of police headquarters.

Black Manny studied the face of the Hispanic man who slid into the front seat of Ito's car.

"Yo, that's the mothafucking narc who's been fucking wit' us for the longest! I don't believe dat nigga's flipping this way!" Three Finger June said with a sinister grin.

Black Manny nodded his head and said, "I told you niggas that boy was riding dirty! A nigga don't just walk away from the game for no reason. He probably got knocked off for some bullshit and flipped on the spot. That's how it always happens. I've seen hardcore niggas upstate playing that same game."

Three Finger June had already decided to eliminate the problem. It was to nobody's benefit to have Ito running his mouth. He knew too much, and once he started pointing fingers, new jails would have to be built, because the list of sinners was long, and Three Finger June, Lil' Bert, and Black Manny were the leading candidates. "Somebody's gotta die!" Three Finger June said with vengeance.

"I feel you, big homie," Black Manny replied.

Once Detective Ruiz got out of Ito's car, Three Finger June and Black Manny followed Ito until he parked at Fairhill and Pike in front of his mother's house. Three Finger June wanted to ambush him right there in front of everybody on the block, not caring if innocent bystanders got shot. Business needed to be handled, and nothing was gonna interfere with their mission. *If a mothafucka wants to play hero, they will get it too.*

But Black Manny had other plans. Shooting Ito was too easy. He wanted to torture his rat ass and bring the bitch out of him. He wanted to cut his tongue out and slide it up his ass. This beef was as personal as it could be. Ito was not only a founder of the Suicidal Riders, he had been second in command, the nigga Black Manny looked up to the most. *I can't believe he's turned snitch!*

Unaware that he was being followed, Ito left his mother's house and went about his daily business, making stops at a Chinese whore parlor, his baby's mom's house, and again with Detective Ruiz.

The more Black Manny watched him, the more his adrenaline increased. He was feeling it. He loved the power he felt when he was about to take a nigga's life. Seven months out of jail, with three bodies under his belt, Black Manny wanted the streets to feel the return of the Hands of Death—Black Manny.

After he met with Detective Ruiz for the second time in one day, Ito decided to put his plan into action. He felt safe and secure with the wire tight at the center of his chest. He placed the phone call he'd wanted to place to his former partner.

"Hello! Who the fuck is this?" Lil' Bert asked, not recognizing the number on his cell phone screen.

"Damn, partner! It's been that long?" Ito asked, trying to figure out if Lil' Bert was acting normally.

"Nah, I just didn't expect you to be calling me, that's all."

"Why not? We still partners, aren't we?"

"Let you tell it!" Lil' Bert rolled his eyes. *Either this nigga's crazy or he's trying to set me up. He's probably sitting next to the po-po, recording this conversation. I've got something for his ass! He wants to play? Let's play! Punk motherfucker forgot who he's fucking with.* He listened to Ito explain his reason for calling.

"For real, partner, I heard what went down between you and MaryLuz, and the reality is that's between you two. I know how she gets. Some bitches need to be put in check."

"Listen, let me make this clear. Nothing went down between MaryLuz and me. Tete and her got into it, and it was a fair fight. She got her ass beat down. Fuck what the streets are saying! But if you want to take this to the next level, then we can!" Lil' Bert was defiant.

"Nah. As I said, that's between you two. She'll be all right. She's a grown woman," Ito said, feeling the anguish in his voice.

"If you want to talk to me, you know where to find me. I got work to do," Bert said, selecting his words carefully just in case Ito was recording the conversation.

"I want my spot back. I'm tired of doing nothing, and I miss the streets. I miss my boys. Plus, my paper's running low. Am I still part of the family?"

"I know plenty of places where they're hiring people with good wages. Ever since ICE started deporting all the Mexicans, a lot of jobs have come open. I'm sure you can find work," Lil' Bert replied, playing stupid.

Ito knew he wasn't supposed to be on the phone talking about the game. Lil' Bert knew it too, and that was why he was being extra careful in choosing his words.

"Stop playing, nigga! I'm for real! I got a boy I been fucking with for a while. He's from Wilmington, and he's interested in copping some serious weight, maybe ten to twenty birds. The boy is sitting on a quarter mil. Now are you interested or not? This'll be easy money."

"Yo, I'm late for work. I'll see you when I see you," Lil' Bert replied.

"How about I come by in a half hour, and we can chill and talk like the old days?"

"Like I said, you know where to find me, partner." Lil' Bert hung up the phone.

Lil' Bert dialed Three Finger June's cell phone.

"Holla at your boy," June said while smoking a fat blunt.

"Ay yo, that nigga Ito just called me. He's on his way over here talking about copping weight and shit. You still on his ass or what?"

"Yeah, we were wondering who he was talking to. Man, that nigga's been running errands all day. He met twice with a punk-ass narc. In fact, we're right across the street from the Round House."

"For real?"

"Yeah, nigga. Your boy has rolled over."

"Make sure you follow that nigga until he gets here. I'm at the stash house on Eighth Street. Make sure he ain't being followed by the po-po. Give me a call when you get here," Lil' Bert said. "'Kill a rat' is the ghetto anthem I live by!" he blared out loudly as he turned the stereo system up.

Ito pulled up in front of Lil' Bert's stash house and could hear the music bumping loud and hard. He was hesitant about going through with his plans. If it didn't work, he'd be dead, but it was either cooperate with the police or go to prison. He failed to spot Black Manny and Three Finger June creeping up beside his car. The next thing he felt was the barrel of Three Finger June's .45 on his temple.

"Nigga, don't make this a homicide! What'cha wanna holler at my boy about?"

"Man, I—"

"Shhh! Don't say nothing!" Black Manny said. He pulled Ito out of his car and pushed him toward the stash house. He jabbed the gun into Ito's kidney and walked him to the door. When they entered the house, Lil' Bert got up from the couch and walked to Ito. He smacked him hard, and suddenly Ito's bladder gave way and he pissed in his pants. "Nigga, you a snitch now, huh?"

"What are you talking about? I'm no snitch! If I were, don't you think you would've been locked up a long time ago with all the dirt we've done together? Man, we killed niggas together! I swear to God, I never crossed you! You my people! I love you—"

"Yo, that nigga's lying! We saw him twice meeting with the narc boy who's been fucking our business up. This nigga's a rat!" Three Finger June said as he slammed the .45 across Ito's head over and over.

After five minutes of a bloody and vicious pistol-whipping, Ito still denied being a snitch.

"Drag this nigga to the basement," Lil' Bert said, hitting Ito one more time with the .45.

Black Manny threw Ito down the steps and walked down behind him. He tied Ito to a steam pipe.

When he saw what Lil' Bert had planned for him, Ito's eyes widened in terror, and his body trembled. "Man, don't do this to me! We boys! What'd I do to deserve this, man? I got mad love for you!"

"Nah, nigga. We used to be boys 'til you turned rat! Now you must pay the price. You know the game," Lil' Bert said. Then he instructed Black Manny and Three Finger June to pull Ito's pants down. Ito tried to kick, but he was powerless. Black Manny held Ito's legs while Three Finger June removed his pants.

Lil' Bert stood over Ito with a pair of pressure pliers in his hands and a smile on his face. "Nigga, you've been found guilty of being a snitch! Nevertheless, I'ma make you believe in this game. You fucked up. You know that, right?" he said as he gripped Ito's nut sack in his hand, pressing the pliers lightly against Ito's nuts.

"Man, I swear I never ratted you or anyone out!"

"I want to know everything you've been sharing with that narc cop. Think before you speak. You only get two chances to lie. For every lie, I'ma crush one of your nuts. Test me if you want." Lil' Bert placed one of Ito's nuts between the pliers. The coldness of the pliers made Ito lose control of his bowels.

"Ohhhh, man. This nigga done shit himself," Black Manny said.

"You nasty," said Three Finger June.

"They don't know shit about us or you! I never said anything about our business! I never told them about the pregnant chick or Pretty Tone, the mailman, or D-Rock. Believe me, they know nothing! That narc keeps harassing me about dumb shit!" Ito was pleading his case in a pitiful way, but his pleas fell on deaf ears.

Lil' Bert picked the shit up and smeared it on Ito's face. "Now they can see the shit." Lil' Bert pressed the pliers with all the strength he had, and there was nothing but skin caught in between the pliers.

Ito drifted into unconsciousness. Forty-five minutes later when he came to, Lil' Bert was standing over him, ready to crush his other nut.

"Lie to me again and you'll lose your other nut! Then you will be a nutless nigga!"

Ito wished they had shot him in the head. The pain was too much to bear. "Man, whatever you want me to do, I'll do!" He knew he needed to plead, beg, and suck dick if they asked him to just to stop the torture. He had taken great joy in torturing other niggas who he believed had been rats. He loved when they screamed and begged for mercy, but never in a million years did he imagine that the tables would turn one day and he would find himself on the receiving end of the stick. He always prided himself on being hardcore, a nigga who could endure endless pain, but he was wrong, and he screamed in agony before he cried and begged for his life.

"How bad do you want to live?" Black Manny, who sat in a chair next to him, asked Ito.

"I thought we were boys! I don't want to die!" Ito cried, coughing up blood.

"I'll tell you what. If you bring that cop friend of yours to us, I'll let you walk away with your life and your one remaining nut," Black Manny said.

"Okay, okay! I'll call him! Give me a phone, please!" Ito said, hoping Black Manny would keep his word.

As he dialed Detective Ruiz's cell number, he closed his eyes and sucked in the pain, but it was too much, so he made up a story about being hurt in a car accident.

"Hello. Detective Ruiz."

"Hey, it's me, Ito. I need your help. I've had a car accident, and I'm hurt bad. I don't want to go to the hospital because they'll ask a lot of questions. You know what I'm talking about. If you take me, they won't ask any questions. Will you come and get me? I'm hurting, man! I'm at a friend's house. The address is 2629 North Eighth Street. Hurry up, please! I'm in pain!"

"I'll be there in five minutes. I'm down on Fifth Street now, at the Cousin Food Market. Are you alone?"

"Yeah, yeah!" Ito replied as Lil' Bert took the phone away from his ear and hung up.

"Duct-tape this nigga!" Lil' Bert ordered Three Finger June.

Once Ito was duct-taped, Lil' Bert pressed the pliers into Ito's remaining nut. Ito immediately passed out. Lil' Bert let go of the pliers, forced Ito's mouth open, and attached the pliers to his tongue. After yanking the pliers several times, Lil' Bert grew frustrated.

Black Manny and Three Finger June both laughed like a house on fire.

"What's so funny, nigga! This punk mothafucka still has a tongue! He don't deserve one!" Lil' Bert said as he tried again to yank Ito's tongue out of his mouth.

"I feel you, homie," Black Manny said as he pulled out the same box cutter he'd used to cut Papo's tongue out. "Hold the pliers tight," he said to Lil' Bert as he began cutting on Ito's tongue with the box cutter.

In less than a minute, Lil' Bert was holding the pliers with Ito's tongue between them as if the tongue were an exotic game trophy. His whole demeanor changed from that of complete frustration to that of a happy man. Without remorse, he watched his childhood best friend die like the dirty rat he was. "Who got the last laugh, mothafucka?" he asked.

Bert didn't know that even in his death, Ito would deny him the last laugh.

It was pitch-black when Detective Ruiz entered the residence of 2629 North Eighth Street. He called out Ito's name, but there was no response. His instincts told him to reach for his gun, and when he did, it wasn't in the holster. He'd left it under the seat in his car as he usually did when he went off duty. He thought about returning to the car and retrieving it, but it was too late. A bullet slammed into the back of his head, and his life was over. Detective Ruiz never felt a thing. His body lay sprawled out on the floor next to Ito's.

Lil' Bert's .45 was still hot from the hollow tip bullet that had just passed through it. "I'm the man, nigga! You see that shit! A dead mothafucking pig! That's my work! I'm claiming that!" Lil' Bert was glowing with excitement. In his mind, a dead cop was just one more motherfucker the city would have to bury and replace.

"What're we gonna do with these two bodies?" Three Finger June asked as he looked anxiously at Lil' Bert.

"Don't panic. I got this," Black Manny said. He started wiping prints off of every surface and item they'd touched. When he was finished, he took the pliers that were lying on top of Ito's chest and shoved them down Ito's throat.

Because it was too risky to move the bodies from the stash house, they lit fires in every room before they disappeared out the back door. When they were a block away, they looked back, and the stash house was up in flames.

When the fire was put out an hour and a half later, police and fire forensic experts discovered the partially burned bodies of two men. The fire marshal searched the clothes of the two victims and made a shocking discovery. The heavy silver badge of Detective Ruiz fell from his wallet and into the charred ashes.

Lieutenant John Smith held Detective Ruiz's identification card in his hand as he stood over the body of his longtime friend. He cleared the room while he searched the pockets of the second victim. He soon discovered a wire taped on the victim's chest, and a miniature tape recorder taped under his armpit.

Chapter Twenty-two

Murder Was the Case That They Gave Me

After Reverend Cruz's death, Chief Jackson and Agent Cleary, the most respected FBI officials in Philadelphia, sat in a conference room trying to figure out how to bring drug-trafficking charges against Fat Angel. They were deeply disappointed that their case against Reverend Cruz and Bolo had ended in such a disaster. This was the one case that had the surefire potential to put their office back on top.

"Damn! We should've arrested those scumbags when we had them. Now they're both dead," Agent Cleary said as he looked at Chief Jackson for some kind of guidance.

"The top brass in Washington couldn't be any more angry, but they'll get over it," Chief Jackson said. "It's a case like this that makes or breaks careers. We still have a very resourceful informant who we can use for some other mission. Let's relocate him to Brick City, New Jersey, and see what he can deliver to us. He'll fit right in with the rest of those low-life drug dealers. It's either that or we charge him up," he barked while he flipped through Reverend Cruz's and Bolo's files. Closing them, he scribbled, "Case closed, deceased," on the front cover of each file.

***

Fat Angel and his lawyer, Charles Fibre, sat in a private office inside the FBI building in Center City, Philadelphia. After forty-five minutes of discussing Angel "Fat Angel" Cruz's agreement to become a paid informant for the Feds, Angel let out a sigh of relief, feeling content and confident now that he knew he wouldn't be seeing the inside of an institution. The way the game was being played nowadays, every other supposedly cold-blooded nigga had started talking once he was put in a no-win position. *Fuck it. I'd rather tell on a motherfucka than be told on! And I'ma get paid, too! Shit is on!* he thought as he signed the agreement papers.

After Agent Cleary explained to Angel that he would be his contact person and that he'd be given a new identity in a few days, Angel was on cloud nine.

Agent Cleary handed Angel a new cell phone and advised him to carry it with him at all times. "This phone has a traceable global positioning system built into it. It lets me know where you are and who you are talking to at all times. Don't lose it, and make all your drug transactions on it. Now tell me, Mr. Cruz. Besides Willie Gomez, what's going to be your street nickname?"

"Twenty."

"Why Twenty?"

"Because it is easy to remember, "Angel said with a smile.

Twenty was the name of an old head who'd been murdered while serving twenty years in the Huntington State Prison in the mountains of central Pennsylvania. He'd been stabbed twenty times over twenty packs of Newports on the twentieth of December. Angel had never met the real Twenty, but he'd heard the jailhouse stories about his life. Now he was stealing his name and a part of his life while he was in the Feds, and now that he had a real opportunity to start his life over with a new identity, Twenty was his new moniker. Fat Angel the rat was officially dead.

Lieutenant John Smith was in tears when he finished listening to the tape he had received from Ito's body. The whole room on the fifth floor of police headquarters was as quiet and solemn as a funeral parlor. The pain of losing one of their own could be felt across the department.

The city's mayor ordered all city buildings to lower their flags to half-mast, and all officers on duty were ordered to wear a black ribbon over their badges. News stations across the Delaware Valley covered the story several times a day.

The entire homicide unit watched the news in shock and disbelief. Off-duty officers, FBI agents, state troopers, and highway patrol officers flooded into the homicide unit. What had been a twenty-man unit was now jammed with over 200 angry cops. One of their own had been killed, and that was all that really mattered.

Police Commissioner Steve Williams broke the silence in the room by ordering all the assembled officers down to the ground floor of the building to a much bigger room. Once the officers had lined up in rows of ten, the commissioner began his tearful speech.

"Ladies and gentlemen, today the department has lost one of its best homicide investigators. Alberto Ruiz was a father, a brother, a friend, and a decorated officer of this department. We don't have any suspects . . . yet! I want every officer in this room to do what is expected to bring the people responsible for this to justice. The department will put all its resources into this investigation. No one, and I mean no one, kills a police officer in this city and gets away with it! I want every drug house, drug corner, and hot spot shut down. I want every parolee in this city accounted for. I want every man and woman out on bail for a gun charge brought in for questioning. We will not sleep until we find the person responsible for this! If you have to kick in doors, kick them in! If you have to violate someone's civil rights, do it! I'll take the heat, but I want whoever did this brought to justice now!

"I want everyone in here to listen to this tape," Williams said, turning on the tape player that he had hooked up to the PA system in the training room.

The demeanor of every officer in the room changed. Some were teary-eyed, some shook uncontrollably, and some held hands and embraced one another as they listened to the last minutes of Detective Alberto Ruiz's life. Once the tape stopped playing, silence fell over the room.

Officer Jonathan Kimmitt, one of the many officers who'd volunteered to work around the clock, recognized one of the names on the tape from his days as a correctional officer at Graterford Prison.

After the police commissioner dismissed the officers, Officer Kimmitt approached him with what was probably the biggest lead in the case. "Sir, as I listened to the tape, I believe I recognized the voice of one of the names mentioned. I'm not sure if it really means anything. However, I'd like your permission to look into it tomorrow morning. The name of the individual mentioned on the tape, Black Manny, sounds like an inmate in Graterford Prison whom I personally had a few run-ins with while working there. As I said, sir, it may not be anything. Nevertheless, I'd like to check it out first thing in the morning."

What Officer Jonathan Kimmitt left out was that he'd been one of the many correctional officers who'd smuggled drugs and cell phones into the prison for Black Manny and that he actually knew that the second unidentified voice on the tape belonged to Lil' Bert. *If I play this right, I could be promoted to plainclothes,* he thought as he stared into the eyes of Police Commissioner Steve Williams.

"Permission granted. Report back to me personally. Lieutenant Smith will travel with you to the prison. Dig up whatever you can on these animals," the police commissioner said, and then he turned around and spoke again into the mic. "Please! Make sure all of you wear your vests at all times!"

Graterford Prison was home to some of Philadelphia's most notorious drug dealers. Miguel "Black Manny" Colon had spent the last five years of his life there. The prison was where Officer Jonathan Kimmitt had become familiar with the worst of the worst from the slums of Philly, and Black Manny was at the top of the list.

Lieutenant Smith and Officer Kimmitt walked up to the main entrance of the prison and identified themselves to the black correctional officer who was at the front desk talking on the phone. She studied Lieutenant Smith's face as if she remembered him from somewhere. "May I help you, sir?"

Both Lieutenant Smith and Officer Kimmitt showed the young correctional officer their identification.

"Okay, I need to put this plastic bracelet on your wrist before I can let you in. An officer will escort you down to security."

Smith and Kimmitt walked down a long corridor and were greeted by the deputy superintendent when they reached the control center. The deputy escorted the two down a flight of stairs to the security office, where he introduced them to Captain Tony Dickski, a short, heavyset white man with a chalky complexion and blotches of freckles that made his face look dirty. He wore Coke-bottle glasses and had a scruffy, dirty beard. The interior of his office was painted a depressing green, and there were dozens of pictures of prison gang members on the wall behind the desk. On another wall were pictures of inmates who were classified as gang leaders and prison organizational leaders. "What can we do for you?" Captain Dickski asked before spitting tobacco juice into a bottle.

"We have every reason to believe that an inmate here named Black Manny may be involved in the murder of Detective Alberto Ruiz. If he is not involved, we think he knows the people who are. We'd like to speak to him." Lieutenant Smith spoke with a warmth in his voice that made Captain Dickski sit straight up in his chair.

"Do you have a full name on this individual?"

"No. All we have is a nickname. That's the reason why we are here," Lieutenant Smith said.

"I recognized the name Black Manny as an individual who was on C-block. I'm not sure of his full name, but I'm sure he was housed on C-unit," Officer Kimmitt said.

After a brief search on the computer, Captain Dickski brought up a prison picture of Miguel "Black Manny" Colon on the screen. "This is the only individual we have in our system with the nickname Black Manny. However, he maxed out his sentence seven months ago. We have no known address or any other information on him. Once a prisoner maxes out, we lose track of him. You can talk to the senior officer on the housing unit where he was housed. Those guys in there know more than us. That's the best I can do. I'm sorry we can't offer more," Captain Dickski said as he picked up the phone and dialed C-unit's extension.

"This is Captain Dickski. Send CO Delsmith to my office ASAP."

Ten minutes later, Jackie Delsmith entered the office, smiling nervously. "You sent for me, Captain?" she asked, fearing she was in some kind of trouble.

"This is Lieutenant Smith and Officer Kimmitt from the Philadelphia Police Department. These gentlemen are conducting an investigation on an individual by the name of Miguel 'Black Manny' Colon. I thought you could help them out," the captain said and spit again into the bottle.

"Officer Delsmith, do you have any idea where we can locate Mr. Colon?" asked Lieutenant Smith.

"Black Manny was released about seven months ago," Officer Delsmith said. "He was very wild. He's what we called stir-crazy. Hung around with a group of guys who called themselves the Suicidal Riders. Should have never been let out of prison. I'm not surprised to learn that he may have been involved in murdering a cop. In fact, I always believed he was responsible for the death of another prisoner here, although we could never prove it. No one would speak to us for fear of this animal. It was only yesterday that he communicated with one of his friends on C-unit. I'm sure of this because I delivered the mail on the CB-2 section, and I saw his name on a letter. The letter was addressed to inmate Sileva, also known as King Unknown."

As Correctional Officer Jackie Delsmith continued telling the Philadelphia police officers what she knew, Captain Dickski dispatched his security boys to King Unknown's cell with instructions to confiscate all mail and photographs found in there.

Twenty minutes later, the Cert Team walked into Captain Dickski's office, carrying a record box filled with mail and photographs. All the contents in the record box were laid out on the table while the two police officers looked at each picture carefully.

"Who's the guy here?" Lieutenant Smith asked, pointing at a picture of Lil' Bert and Black Manny, flashing what appeared to be money in one hand and guns in the other.

"He's the leader of the gang Black Manny ran with," Delsmith said. "He's the same person who picked him up the day he was released." Jackie was throwing dirt in the game. She knew this was her chance to get even with Black Manny and Lil' Bert for what they'd done to her. At that moment, she felt no remorse about the abortion she'd been forced to get. She couldn't wait to see Manny's face when they brought him back to the 'Ford.

"Captain, can we have a copy of this photograph and this letter? And by the way, does anybody know this other individual's name?" Lieutenant Smith asked, pointing at Lil' Bert's picture.

"I believe he goes by the name of Bert, Lil' Bert . . . something like that. Many of the Hispanic guys in here look up to him as though he were some kind of god," Jackie Delsmith said with a smile.

"What'd you say his name was?" Lieutenant Smith asked again, feeling hopeful and confident that they were on to something.

"They call him Lil' Bert. Something like that," Jackie Delsmith repeated.

Lieutenant Smith and Officer Kimmitt looked at each other in disbelief. Now they could put a face to the two scumbags on the tape they'd recovered from the unidentified body that had lain next to Detective Ruiz.

Lieutenant Smith had a feeling in the pit of his stomach that he had the right person. It was more than just a coincidence that the ex-prisoner and Bert had the same nicknames as the people who'd been mentioned on the tape.

"If it will help, you can have a copy of this." Captain Dickski played a video showing Lil' Bert waiting in front of the prison for Black Manny to be released.

After the video ended, Correctional Officer Delsmith broke the silence. "I have a question. Is there a reward for the capture of the suspects?" she asked, looking directly at the police lieutenant.

"Yes, seventy-five thousand dollars," he said. "And who knows? Maybe you two can try to claim it. We'll be in touch," he said as he got up to leave Captain Dickski's office.

Back in North Philly, homicide detectives rounded up dozens of Hispanic men around Eighth Street and brought them in for questioning. Other detectives conducted door-to-door interviews of residences in search of witnesses. The grind up was in full effect. The streets of Philly were put on notice. A cop killer was on the loose, and no one would walk the streets in peace until someone was arrested.

Commissioner Steve Williams waited anxiously for the arrival of Lieutenant Smith and Officer Kimmitt with the information and potential evidence they had from the visit to Graterford Prison. News stations around the city crammed in front of the Round House, waiting for the news conference Williams had promised them.

An hour later, Lieutenant Smith and Officer Kimmitt arrived at the Round House. When they stepped off the elevator, the entire homicide unit grew quiet. Smith and Kimmitt held evidence that they hoped would break the case.

Police Commissioner Steve Williams studied the information, then stepped to the main floor of the unit. He held up two eight-by-ten photos, one in each hand.

"These are our suspects. They are armed and dangerous. We have every reason to believe they're still in the city. Every lead must be followed. Bring these bastards in dead or alive! I want this case solved now! At twelve this afternoon a press conference will be held. By then, every officer in the city will have a copy of the suspects' photos. At one p.m., SWAT will conduct searches at the locations the suspects are believed to be at. Again, these suspects should be considered armed and dangerous!"

Chapter Twenty-three

My Last Wish

Lil' Bert was agitated. He'd been at his mother's house, listening to her ramble on after seeing his picture splashed all over the news.

"I knew you were no good. Look at you up there." She pointed to the TV. "Wanted for murder. A real tough man you are. Real men don't need to murder to gain respect. They earn it. Where did I go wrong with you?"

"I don't want to hear it right now," he said. Her nagging was making him increasingly uncomfortable.

"I oughta turn your ass in. Get me that reward money. You ain't never take care of me like you should."

"I gave you plenty."

"Bertito, I need fifty dollars to buy a few bags. I'm sick! Fifty dollars is way less than what the police are offering for you. Don't you see that I'm sick, *cabron?* I need a fix now!"

Uncertain of his mother's threats, Lil' Bert considered putting a bullet right between her eyes, but he settled on restraining his rage. He had come to her house with a mission in mind. "Mom, you'd turn your own son into the police?" He shook his head and grinned in anticipation of his mission.

"*Hijoito,* son, I know I could never call myself a mother. I've been a dopefiend ever since I was fifteen years old. My whole life has been centered around drugs. I'm sorry I could never give you the love every son needs and deserves from his mother. My worth as a mother is nothing. But I still love you. We may not see eye to eye, but it's my blood running through your veins. Whether you like it or not, I gave birth to you, and I'm the reason you are who you are today. I tried my best to give you all the love you needed. It's not my fault your father didn't want to claim you. That son of a bitch never did anything for you!" Damaris was hoping her sad spiel would touch Lil' Bert's heart and he would break her off with some cash. She never stopped with her hustle for more dope.

"I really don't give a fuck about my father, so I wish you would stop mentioning him! As far as I'm concerned, I don't have a father or a mother! If I saw him right now, I swear I'd kill him! Fuck him, you, and anyone who's concerned about him! The streets raised me. The drug game is my father!" Lil' Bert's words were alive and full of pain, a kind of pain that can only be replaced with violence.

"I'm sorry, baby! I'm sorry for not being a mother to you. I'm so sorry—"

"Nah, you ain't sorry about not being there for me. You're only sorry when you want something from me."

"No, I'm really sorry. I don't know how much time I have in this world. I have terminal cancer, and Dr. Torres informed me I only have two to four months to live. There's nothing they can do for me," said Damaris, sitting down next to Lil' Bert.

Don't worry, you junkie-ass bitch! Lil' Bert thought. *You don't have to wait two to four months to meet your Maker.* He could hardly contain himself as he reached into his pocket and pulled out three bags of dope, tossing them in his mother's lap. He watched his mother glow with excitement as she scooped them up.

She pulled out a filthy syringe, cracked open the three bags of dope, and poured the powder into a rusty soda cap, adding a couple of drops of water. Her hands shook as she lit the lighter and guided the flame under the cap. When the dope was dissolved, she drew it up into the filthy syringe. She turned her head to one side, and adroitly stuck the needle into her neck vein. When she hit the vein, she pushed the plunger all the way home and fell to the dirty floor like a rag doll. She shook in convulsions as the rat poison took effect.

Lil' Bert smiled as he watched the thick white bubbles foaming in his mother's mouth. Damaris died with the syringe still stuck in her neck.

Unbeknownst to Lil' Bert, Lizzet Santiago, Damaris's crack-whore friend, had seen Bert enter Damaris's house and placed a call to the Philadelphia police. Within minutes, Franklin Street turned into organized chaos as uniformed officers responded to the call. These were officers who were out to play the hero.

After sealing off Franklin Street, SWAT arrived and took positions on rooftops directly across the street from Damaris's house.

Police personnel and Police Commissioner Williams stayed calm, patiently waiting for the SWAT team to enter the house. The cops understood that this was by far the most important lead of their entire investigation. If this panned out, it would be the end of the search for a cop killer.

Commissioner Williams gave the order. "All units move in." The SWAT team moved into position. The lead agent was poised with the battering ram. Just as he was about to swing it forward, the front door opened up. The agent stopped in mid-swing.

Lil' Bert walked out of his mother's house as if nothing had ever happened inside.

"Freeze! Get on the ground!" a detective yelled at Lil' Bert as he came face-to-face with him. The detective aimed his gun at Lil' Bert's chest.

"Shoot me, you punk mothafucking bitch! I'm ready to die! This is a day of triumph for me! Shoot me!"

"Get on the ground now!" another cop yelled.

"Fuck you! You're gonna have to kill me!" Lil' Bert thought about his options and decided to go out like a true gangster. He reached for the gun that was tucked in his waist, but before he could pull it out, every cop on Franklin Street fired his or her guns at him.

"Stop shooting! Stop shooting!" Commissioner Williams shouted. As he stood over Lil' Bert's body, he wondered why Bert wasn't bleeding. Then he realized that Bert was wearing a bulletproof vest that had absorbed the blows of the shots. Only two bullets entered Lil' Bert's right hand. He pressed his knee in the back of Lil' Bert's neck. "You lucky animal! Give me a reason to kill you! Give me a reason!" he said as he cuffed Lil' Bert's wrists.

"You can't kill me! You can't kill me!" Lil' Bert yelled as he was being dragged into a police wagon. When the paddy wagon door was secured, three detectives beat him all the way to Temple University Hospital.

Inside Damaris's house, Lieutenant Smith drew a chalk diagram around Damaris's body. Years of experience told him that her death was a homicide. The evidence was in the three little bags he was holding in his hands. He knew that a young man like Lil' Bert could easily create a motive to assassinate a cop. But it was quite another thing to end the life of the person who had brought him into this world, his own mother.

After a three-hour search of Damaris's house, the only evidence worth taking were a postal mailbag with mail in it that was found under the kitchen sink and the filthy syringe they recovered sticking out of Damaris's neck.

***

At Fifth Street and Indiana Avenue that afternoon, PPD, FBI, DEA, and ATF had Tete's house and the entire block surrounded. People gathered on the corner, waiting for the drama to unfold. After what occurred on Franklin Street earlier, they wondered if they would be treated to some real, live action in broad daylight. Everybody wanted to know who the police were coming to arrest. Whoever it was had to be a major player, because it wasn't every day that the FBI, DEA, and ATF appeared in North Philly.

"This is the police! Come out with your hands up!" a black police officer shouted through a bullhorn.

Tete screamed at Black Manny, who was sleeping buck naked in bed. "Manny! Manny! Get the fuck up! The police have the place surrounded!"

Tete's words struck Black Manny like a punch in the face. "What?" he yelled. He reached for his gun on the nightstand next to the bed. *Damn! I ain't going back to prison! Fuck that!*

He got dressed quickly and put on a bulletproof vest. He peeled the curtain back and looked out the window. He couldn't comprehend the scene at first. Never in his life had he seen so many cops in one place. Any hope of escaping was dead. His only option was to surrender or bang it out with all those pigs. He had enough ammunition to put up a good fight.

"This is the police! Come out with your hands on top of your head!"

Black Manny looked at Tete, who was shaking and crying. At that moment, he couldn't decide whether to kick her out the front door or throw her ass out the second-floor window. "Bitch, you got two choices," he said. "Jump out the window or get thrown the fuck out of it! Pick one!"

That was all Tete needed to hear. She dove headfirst out the second-floor window, landing right in front of her row-house door. She was unconscious and broken up, but that didn't matter to the two FBI agents who dragged her out of the line of fire and slapped handcuffs on her.

No sooner had they gotten Tete into an ambulance than Black Manny let loose from the same window Tete had jumped from moments ago. As soon as he finished emptying one clip, he quickly reloaded, moved away from the window, and took a position at the side window, where he quickly caught two detectives trying to sneak in. He opened fire, blasting one of the detectives dead in the face.

"Officer shot! Officer shot!" the other detective shouted as he dragged his partner away from the house and took cover behind an unmarked police car. Suddenly, all gunfire stopped.

The afternoon turned into evening, and the police shut off the water and electricity in the house. They illuminated the area with powerful spotlights.

It was with mixed emotions that Black Manny faced this evening. With two full clips remaining, he decided to end the standoff. He felt like an actor in a blockbuster movie. He had the crowd on standby. But he wasn't satisfied with his role so far. It was time to try to take out some cops before they roasted his ass.

He crawled from the back hall to the living room, where he yelled out, "I'm coming out! I'm coming out!" Then he threw a gun out the window.

Black Manny appeared to be possessed. There was no stopping him. He was determined to hold court right then and there. There was no point in continuing what had become a soliloquy.

The police again urged Black Manny to surrender.

"I'm coming, mothafuckas! I'm coming!" Black Manny yelled as he squeezed the trigger of his .45 until the clip was empty.

The snipers' bullets hit Manny right between his eyes. His brain splattered all over Tete's living room.

News of Black Manny's death traveled fast in the streets of Philly. Believing he was next to be arrested, Three Finger June decided to turn himself in.

Three Finger June walked through the doors of the police precinct with his head held high. The officer at the reception desk put his hand on his holster, ready for something to pop off. He knew Three Finger June and the ease by which he would use his gun. Other officers slowly came from behind the desk, all ready to open fire.

"No need for any fireworks. I'm here to confess."

The police were in complete shock but still not convinced June was there peacefully.

"I was there when that cop was killed," said Three Finger June.

"Which officer? Detective Ruiz?" the staff sergeant asked.

"I guess that's his name. The narc who was just killed who y'all are going crazy about."

"Put your hands up."

Three Finger June did as he was told. An officer cuffed him and escorted him to an interrogation room.

Three Finger June proceeded to tell the detectives everything that happened that day.

"Will you write all of this down?" The detective handed him a pen and paper.

Three Finger June wrote a twenty-five-page statement. As he finished his statement, the DA arrived.

"Would you be willing to testify against Lil' Bert in court?"

"Gladly." Three Finger June smiled.

"Good. I think we'll be able to take care of you and get you a reduced sentence for your cooperation." The DA couldn't believe his luck.

Chapter Twenty-four

Guilty As Charged

After the doctors released him from Temple University Hospital, Lil' Bert was escorted under heavy guard to the CFCF county jail at 7:30 p.m. He was stripped naked, handcuffed, and shackled. The pain in his arms was excruciating, and the CO was enjoying himself as he placed his nightstick in the center of Lil' Bert's back.

"Do we have a problem?" the CO asked Bert, looking for a reason to beat his ass while he was handcuffed and shackled.

Damn! This cracker thinks he's gonna get it off on me! Bert thought as he listened to the police officers tell the COs that he was a high-profile case and to place him in solitary confinement.

For the next hour and a half, Lil' Bert was the center of attention as a parade of COs passed by and made smart remarks toward him. Later, he was led into an office where a dozen COs were standing around.

Lil' Bert was immediately annoyed and asked, "Is this what a mothafucka goes through when he comes to jail, or do you assholes just enjoy watching a nigga's dick hang?"

The COs studied Lil' Bert's face, while a heavyset, foul-smelling Hispanic lieutenant calmly said, "Mr. Ruiz, my name is Lieutenant Vega. You are being placed in solitary confinement for your safety. You are a special case, and we can't put you in general population. We don't care what you're being detained for. Our responsibility is to keep you alive and well. Do you understand me? Do you have any questions?" Lieutenant Vega asked.

"Nah, I don't have anything to say," Bert replied.

"All right. Now that we have an understanding, I'm going to run down the rules to you so there'll be no misunderstandings. You are not allowed any visits for the first thirty days. You will be placed in solitary confinement until your arraignment. The only visits you are allowed are with your attorney. You are allowed one monitored phone call a week. Do you have any questions?"

"Nah."

"Okay. Get dressed." Lieutenant Vega instructed a CO to uncuff Lil' Bert so he could get dressed.

Once Lil' Bert slipped into an oversized orange jumpsuit, he was again handcuffed and then escorted down a long corridor to the super-max section of the jail. Inside the housing unit, he was stunned by the noise.

"Mr. Ruiz, you are on suicide watch for the next seventy-two hours. During that time, you are not allowed to have anything that you can use to harm yourself or others. It's standard procedure," Lieutenant Vega said, his eyes fixed on Bert and making it obvious to the other guards standing around that he wanted to beat the shit out of Lil' Bert. "Do we have a problem here?" Vega said as he pushed Bert inside the cell, slamming his head up against the wall. "I pray you have a problem so I can shove this nightstick down your fucking throat! Give me a reason, *maricon!*" he yelled.

Once Lil' Bert was secured in his cell, he wondered about Black Manny and Three Finger June and if they had been arrested. He didn't have to wonder for long, for when the shift changed, a CO came to his door and told him the news about how Black Manny had shot it out with the police, killing one and wounding two others before they shot him dead.

Lil' Bert smiled and said nothing. *At least my nigga went out like a real gangster,* he thought as he lay down on the dirty mattress, drifting off into a deep sleep.

It seemed to start almost immediately. He didn't even know what he was dreaming.

It was almost as if he were another person, someone not quite alive. His eyes were open, and he was staring at the ceiling. He could hear the sound of running water from the sink.

Lil' Bert stood and looked out the cell door, and it was pitch dark. In fact, there was no sign of another prison cell in sight. It was as if he were seeing the planet before human beings had ever inhabited it.

The water continued to run in the sink. Anger and hatred penetrated his soul. It was still dark, and then he saw a small ray of light. He was confused, for he couldn't tell where the light was coming from. He forced his eyes to follow the direction of the light. He was afraid that if he started to walk toward the light, it would be days before he reached it.

The light seemed to beckon him. "You will go forward 'til you reach the other end!"

Bert followed the light until he reached the end of it. He stepped into the room where the light was coming from and realized he was at his old stash house on Eighth Street. He could see his reflection bouncing off the walls as he stared at Ito's body, which lay next to the detective he'd slumped.

"Look!" a voice said. It was neither male nor female, but it was a sad voice.

"I'm not afraid to look!" Bert answered. He stared at both dead bodies lying side by side, and all he saw was a

reflection of himself lying next to Ito. The smell of death, of morbid decay, pierced his nostrils. He wanted to scream, but he felt like he was choking. When he looked again at the bodies on the floor, he saw a face—a face he didn't recognize, a face that resembled his. "But I'm not dead!" he screamed.

Lil' Bert sat bolt upright in the bed, his eyes wide open. It took him a moment to realize where he was—in CFCF county jail. "What a fucking nightmare!" he whispered.

At the arraignment the following morning, Lil' Bert pleaded not guilty. The DA promised the judge that he would prove Lil' Bert was guilty as charged. As expected, bail was denied.

After speaking with his lawyer, Lavelle Davis, Lil' Bert realized that his life might be over.

"Mr. Ruiz, I'm going to be straight with you. The district attorney is seeking the death penalty. I don't believe we can plead. We're talking about eight counts of first-degree murder. I haven't had the opportunity to view all the prosecutor's evidence against you, but I have every reason to believe there is a recording of you and your friends committing the murder of Detective Ruiz. To be quite honest, I'm not sure there's anything we can do to avoid the death penalty. There are statements made by witnesses who pinpointed you and put you at the crime scene. The district attorney has enough evidence to win a conviction. I will fight for you, but it doesn't look good," Attorney Davis said as she handed Lil' Bert copies of the statements that had been made against him.

Attorney Davis could see that Lil' Bert was not concerned or fazed by the news she had just given him. "By the way, the DA is pushing for a speedy trial, meaning that we'll be going to trial within the next six months. I can try to cut a deal with the DA for life in prison. That's the best I can do for you."

"Nah, fuck that!" Bert said. "I have the right to a trial by a jury of my peers. I got nothing to lose."

"You certainly do have that right," the attorney replied. She studied his face for a moment, looking for any trace of remorse, but she couldn't find any. "Okay, Mr. Ruiz, I'll be back in a few days so we can start preparing your defense. Should you change your mind about a deal for life in prison, give me a call," she said as she got up from her chair and walked out of the interview room.

Lavelle Davis knew there wasn't much she had to do to prepare for a trial. It was an open-and-shut case. *The fool has no clue what he's gotten himself into, but it's his choice and his right to go to trial,* she thought as she walked out of the jail and into the waiting car where Philadelphia Police Lieutenant Smith and the notorious and vicious District Attorney Roger Dean sat waiting for her.

"Did he confess?" asked Roger Dean as Davis slid into the back seat.

"No. He wants to go to trial."

"All right. There'll be no deal. He deserves the death penalty," Lieutenant Smith said as he drove toward State Road, heading back to police headquarters.

"We're charging this asshole under the 1988 Cop Killer Crime Bill, which makes this a federal case. By doing so, we won't have to deal with him for the next twenty years while he sits and appeals his case on the state's death row. The Feds will fry his ass within three. The rest of the charges will be filed with the State," Roger Dean announced.

"Sounds good to me," Attorney Davis said.

For years, District Attorney Roger Dean and various court-appointed attorneys had been trading cases. He would throw Attorney Lavelle Davis a few petty, meatball cases to win, and in return, she would make sure she sold out the high-profile cases that came her way. Theirs was a symbiotic relationship. Between Attorney Lavelle Davis and DA Roger Dean, they were responsible for putting 249 individuals on Pennsylvania's death row.

On January 10, 2008, the stage was set for one of the biggest murder trials in Philadelphia's history. The Criminal Justice Center at 1301 Filbert Street had been transformed into an ocean of law enforcement officials seeking justice for one of their own. Police officers from as far away as New York City came to glare at Alberto "Lil' Bert" Ruiz and watch his murder trial take place. The public and reporters were banned from the proceedings. Only law enforcement officials and the victim's family were allowed inside the courtroom.

Lil' Bert scanned the courtroom and locked eyes with Detective Ruiz's mother, Maria Vasquez Ruiz. For a brief moment, he felt a deep connection with the old lady. He could see the hurt in her eyes. It was the first time that he felt any emotion toward another human. Sensing a crack in his tough emotional armor, he looked away before any emotions penetrated his mind. He tried to stay focused, but Mrs. Ruiz's stare burned right through him.

He decided to focus his gaze on the empty witness stand. Who were the rats who would testify against him? *It's me against all these motherfuckas.* He knew no one would be in the courtroom to support him. He looked over his shoulder and saw the old lady staring at him, and he quickly turned back around.

When the judge entered the courtroom, everyone stood up except for Lil' Bert. "All should be seated and come to order!" the bailiff announced.

"Good morning," said the elderly, blue-eyed judge. This judge alone had been frying blacks and Hispanics in the City of Brotherly Love for over twenty-five years. Judge Tommy Sebo's reputation could be summed up in three words: the Hanging Judge. "You may proceed, Mr. Dean."

"Thank you, Your Honor. This is the case of Alberto 'Lil' Bert' Ruiz, who has no relation to the victim, Detective Alberto Ruiz. Detective Ruiz was a twenty-seven-year, decorated police officer in the city of Philadelphia. The defendant was arrested on August 5, 2007, for three counts of first-degree murder. That was subsequently upgraded to eight counts of murder. The Commonwealth is seeking the death penalty in this case due to the aggravated circumstances of a murder committed during the course of a felony." District Attorney Roger Dean was prepared to end the case right there.

"Your Honor, if I may, I'd like to have a few minutes to speak to my client," Attorney Davis said.

"You certainly can, Ms. Davis," the judge responded.

Bert's attorney leaned over to him and unfolded the note the district attorney had given her.

Plead here and now to life in prison, and I won't seek the death penalty. You have five minutes to decide.

"What do you want to do, Mr. Ruiz?" Attorney Davis asked as she placed the note in front of him.

"Fuck a plea! Do your job!" Lil' Bert whispered in her ear.

The makeup of the jury came down to ten whites and two Hispanics, ranging from late thirties to late fifties in age. They stared at Lil' Bert with contempt in their eyes before the trial even started.

"Good morning, ladies and gentlemen of the jury. The evidence in this case will show that this man, Alberto 'Lil' Bert' Ruiz, murdered a police officer in cold blood. The evidence that you will hear in this courtroom will show that this man is a cold-blooded killer. He killed people for no reason at all." DA Roger Dean stared at the jurors with tears in his eyes. After a few seconds, he continued, "Today, you will hear about how this man murdered a police officer, a pregnant mother, a postal worker, a police informant, and his own mother. You will hear first from a witness who was present when most of these murders took place, a close friend of Mr. Ruiz's. Ladies and gentlemen, you have an obligation after hearing the evidence to find this defendant guilty as charged!" Dean said, then took a seat at the table.

"Attorney Davis, do you have an opening statement?" the judge asked.

"Thank you, Your Honor. Ladies and gentlemen, the defendant in this case is no angel, but he is not a killer, let alone a cop killer. I ask you to base your decision on the evidence, or the lack of evidence presented here today, and not on your emotions. Thank you."

"The prosecution calls its first witness to the stand. Mr. Jose 'Three Finger June' Rivera, would you state your name for the record and jury please," Mr. Dean stated.

"Jose Rivera," Three Finger June stated. Lil' Bert stared at June with pure venom.

June cleared his throat and prepared to go to work on behalf of the district attorney. He refused to look at Lil' Bert. He had studied his testimony over a dozen times with the DA, to the point where he could spit it like a 50 Cent rap.

Maria Vasquez Ruiz, Ruiz's mother, kept her eyes on Lil' Bert's back. To her, the more she stared at him, the more Lil' Bert resembled her own son. Then all of her unwelcome visions, she knew, were from her son, Detective Ruiz. She could hear his voice calling her.

"Mom, look at your grandson . . . my son. Do you see him? Does he look like me?"

Things were becoming clear to her now. Her own breath now dragged in and out of her lungs as cold as a winter frost. She knew he was dead, so when he held out his hand for her, she didn't panic. He gestured for her to follow him to the defendant's table.

Standing in front of the defendant's table, her face became twisted in a mask of grotesque pain. "Stop!" she shrieked. She couldn't go through it again. "No! This can't be!" For a moment, the pain in her face vanished, and then came the sorrow. She whispered silent words, "I finally found my grandson. No!" Maria screamed inside herself.

"Yes, I am. No matter what you think, I'm your blood, the only link to your son . . . my father."

Lil' Bert's haunting voice made Maria's heart race, and she thought she would faint. "Oh God, help me understand this, please! Help!" She took a long, deep breath and let it out slowly. At that moment, all the hatred she had felt for the accused cop killer dissolved from her heart. Slowly, she backed away from the defendant's table, confused and distressed. "He's not my grandson! He's not my grandson!" Her screams seemed to come from a distance.

"He is my son!" Detective Ruiz said, looking his mother in the eyes as he released her hand.

"Alberto, please don't go! Please don't go!" Maria said as she watched her son disappear from her vision. She looked at the ceiling hoping to see her son again.

"It's okay, Mom. I feel better now that you found my son."

Detective Ruiz may have been dead, but Maria heard his voice in the courtroom. "No!"

She came to with the sound of Three Finger June's powerful voice echoing through the courtroom. Tears of joy and pain fell from her eyes. *I must be hallucinating!* thought Maria as she listened to Three Finger June give his testimony.

"Mr. Rivera, have you ever been arrested before?" Roger Dean asked, smiling devilishly.

"Yes."

"For what?"

"Selling dope."

"For the record, how old are you?"

"Twenty-two."

"What were the results of the charges against you in your past legal matters?"

"I beat the case. The charges were dropped, dismissed."

"Are you familiar with the defendant in this case?"

Looking at Lil' Bert with delight and pleasure, he cleared his throat and replied, "Yes, I am."

"For the record, can you point out the defendant in this case for the jury?"

Without hesitation, June pointed directly at Lil' Bert.

I shoulda slumped that nigga a long time ago. How can he look at himself in the mirror? Lil' Bert thought.

"Let the record show the witness has identified the defendant. Mr. Rivera, I direct your memory to the night of August 5, 2007. Can you tell the judge and jury what transpired that night that brings us here today to this courtroom?"

Three Finger June took a sip of water and then recounted how he and Black Manny had followed Ito around for three days under the instruction of Lil' Bert. He detailed how they'd tortured Ito with the pressure pliers, and how Lil' Bert had crushed Ito's nuts one at a time. When June reached the climax of his testimony, he allowed a tear to escape from the corner of his eye. "I told him not to kill the cop. But no! He came up with a scheme to lure the cop boy to the stash house, and then he shot him in the back of the head!" His performance was worth an Academy Award. By the time he was finished, everyone on the jury was in tears.

"Your Honor, I now submit to you and offer into evidence exhibit A, a tape recording of the last words of Detective Ruiz, a decorated officer of this city." Roger Dean looked toward the jury box and studied the faces of the jury. He had them right where he wanted them—on the edge of their seats.

"Ladies and gentlemen, if at any moment this tape becomes too much to bear, please feel free to inform the judge, and we can have a recess," he said. After a brief pause, he turned on the tape player.

"Hello. Detective Ruiz."

" Hey, it's me, Ito. I need your help. I've had a car accident, and I'm hurt bad. I don't want to go to the hospital because they'll ask a lot of questions. You know what I'm talking about. If you take me, they won't ask any questions. Will you come and get me? I'm hurting, man! I'm at a friend's house. The address is 2629 North Eighth Street. Hurry up, please! I'm in pain!"

District Attorney Roger Dean stopped the tape player, turned toward the jury, and said, "This next excerpt contains the last seconds of Detective Ruiz's life." He pushed the play button. Pow! The sound of a gunshot blared through the speakers. There was an eerie silence in the room, and then a voice followed the sound of the gunshot.

"I'm the man, nigga! You see that shit! A mothafucking dead pig! That's my work! I'm claiming that!"

"Ladies and gentlemen, that voice you just heard belongs to this defendant, Alberto 'Lil' Bert' Ruiz," District

Attorney Roger Dean whispered while pointing at Lil' Bert, who was smiling.

For the next hour and a half, the prosecution gave the jury a detailed account of the eight murders Lil' Bert was charged with. Not once did Bert's attorney make an objection.

"Ladies and gentlemen, this man is so evil that he murdered his own mother! I submit that he deserves nothing less than the ultimate penalty, the death penalty. Anything less than a first-degree verdict will be an injustice to the community, to this city, to this police department, and most of all, to the family of Detective Ruiz. They deserve justice!"

The DA turned to the judge and said, "Your Honor, at this point the Commonwealth rests."

"Ms. Davis, would you like to address the court on behalf of your client?" the judge asked.

"Yes, Your Honor. Ladies and gentlemen, you heard the testimony of Mr. Rivera. You heard the tape recording of Detective Ruiz's last moments on this earth. My client is no angel, but he is not the monster Mr. Dean made him out to be. He's a young man who was abandoned by both his mother and father. He started living on the streets at the age of thirteen. His mother was a drug addict who left him in crackhouses while she ran the streets. Yes, he did a lot of bad things in his life to survive in the mean streets of Philadelphia. This young man needs help, lots of it. If you pay attention, not once did Detective Ruiz identify himself as a police officer. Not once did the prosecution's star witness, Mr. Rivera, make any reference to Detective Ruiz identifying himself. So the question you must ask yourself is this: was this crime premeditated murder? My client deserves the benefit of the doubt in this case. Thank you."

Attorney Davis patted Lil' Bert on the back as she took her seat beside him. Bert seemed satisfied with her performance.

The jury took only forty-five minutes to return with a verdict. Lil' Bert was escorted from the holding cell back into the courtroom.

Once the jury was bought back into the courtroom and seated, Judge Sebo inquired, "Has the jury reached a verdict?"

"Yes, Your Honor, we have," responded the jury foreman.

The bailiff passed the judge the verdict note, and the courtroom went completely silent as the judge read the verdict to himself. He looked first at the prosecutor and then at Lil' Bert, and he ordered the defendant to rise.

Lil' Bert again decided to remain seated while his attorney stood at attention. Completely surrounded by detectives and courtroom officers, Bert looked stoic as Judge Sebo read the verdict.

"Mr. Ruiz, the jury has found you guilty of murder in the first degree in the killing of Detective Alberto Ruiz. This court is mandated by law to impose upon you the maximum sentence, which is death by lethal injection. Mr. Ruiz, you are a despicable individual, and no civilized society deserves you among them. You killed a police officer. You hurt people because you have no idea what life is about. You have failed to show even a modicum of remorse or responsibility for your actions. It is the obligation of the court to turn you over to the custody of the Department of Corrections until such time as the Commonwealth carries out the sentence imposed by this court. It is so ordered!" Judge Sebo said.

Immediately, the officers rushed Lil' Bert out of the courtroom.

Maria Vasquez Ruiz stared at Lil' Bert as he was being led away. For a moment, they looked intently at each other, and at that instant, Maria knew that this convicted murderer, Alberto "Lil' Bert" Ruiz, was indeed her grandson.

Chapter Twenty-five

Death Row

A year later, Lil' Bert found himself on Graterford Prison's J-block, better known as death row, as the rest of the prison population called it. J-block was a hellhole, a modern-day slave plantation where 98 men, mostly Hispanics and Blacks, awaited their fate.

On a daily basis, Lil' Bert put up with the insults from the correctional officers who had friends and family members who were police officers. They despised a cop killer. Among the other condemned men, Lil' Bert was a hero, the one not to be disrespected.

Shortly after his arrival, the other death-row prisoners nicknamed him Cop Killa, a nickname he embraced with pride.

Even in the most secure section of the prison, Lil' Bert managed to have his way. Within two months of arriving on death row, he was making moves with some of the remaining members of the Suicidal Riders in the general population, and soon J-block was flooded with marijuana and dope. Members of the Suicidal Riders regularly packed his food tray with everything he requested, even managing to get a cell phone to him, and that was how he managed to get MaryLuz back into his life.

MaryLuz, on the other hand, was planning on taking Lil' Bert for all his stash money. *The mothafucka got to pay for what he did to me,* she thought as she prepared to pick up all of Bert's worldly possessions. Once she picked up his stash, she was excited to know that he had $350,000. As her last act of payback, she took to the district attorney all the letters he had written to her confessing to killing Reverend Cruz and Bolo.

Lil' Bert was getting impatient as the hours went by and his cell was not called for a visit. "Where the fuck this bitch is at?" he said, stressing himself out. The visiting hours came and went, and he was feeling the reality of the situation.

When the CO came around passing the mail out, he was excited to receive a letter from MaryLuz.

> *Dear Bert:*
> *I will keep this one short. I just wanted you to know that God don't like ugly. You have been played, nigga! Thanks for the money. I surely feel better now.*
> *Kisses and hugs!*
> *P.S. I pray you suffer a painful death!*

Lil' Bert was at his breaking point. No money, no girl, and no lawyer. The only things that kept him connected to the streets were his cell phone and his pen pal, Website. He made sure his closest associates on the row had access to the phone. He understood the power a simple letter from the outside world had on a condemned man. He enjoyed seeing the other prisoners standing at their cell doors waiting for the guard to deliver mail.

A year and a day after arriving on death row, Bert sat in his cell writing letters when the mail officer stopped at his door.

"Ruiz, mail!" the redneck guard yelled.

"Throw that shit on the floor. I'll get it," Bert replied.

When the guard walked away from his door, Bert stood quickly and snatched up the five pieces of mail the guard had dropped into his cell. He didn't recognize the name and return address on the first letter he picked up, and he was immediately curious. *Damn! It's probably a new pen pal!* he thought as he opened the letter.

> *Dear Alberto:*
> *I hope this letter finds you well. I understand you have no idea who I am and why I'm writing to you. Truthfully, my feelings and emotions are mixed, and my life is in a complete transition. This may come as a surprise to you, but I am your biological grandmother, Maria Vasquez Ruiz, and you are my only grandson. I will understand if you decide you don't want to correspond with me after reading this letter. But I want you to know that I forgive you for what you've done, and I would very much like to be a part of your life and support you in whatever way I can. I pray you will write me back. I am including my house phone number. Please feel free to call.*
> *I pray to meet you in person someday soon if you'd like. Enclosed is a picture of your biological father. He searched for you for many years, and when he finally located you, it was too late. You were on the opposite side of the law, and he was on your trail.*
> *Love, your grandmother,*
> *Maria Vasquez Ruiz*

For a long while, Lil' Bert thought the letter was some kind of cruel joke. He removed the photo from the envelope and stared incredulously at the face of the man who had brought him into this world, the man he had murdered in cold blood, Detective Alberto Martinez-Melendez Ruiz.

Chapter Twenty-six

Blood Is Thicker Than Water

Lil' Bert paced back and forth in his cell, awaiting his visit. Today was the day he was formally meeting his grandmother, Maria Vasquez Ruiz, in person. He had gone over everything he was going to tell her. He no longer had to pretend that he was not notorious. His name still flew around North Philly like a Tupac song.

Maria Vasquez Ruiz had done her homework, and for the past year after Lil' Bert's murder trial, she had made it her business to retrace his upbringing. What she found was a disturbing picture of neglect, child abuse, and abandonment, which broke her heart into millions of pieces. By the time she was done looking into Lil' Bert's upbringing, she knew she had to stand by him through thick and thin. She understood where his anger was coming from, and she wanted to help heal him and teach him to let go of hate.

Maria wondered how a mother could leave her child in a crackhouse for days while she went out whoring. If anyone were to blame for her son's death, it would have to be her son, Detective Ruiz, for being involved with a worthless piece of shit such as Damaris Martinez.

There was no mystery involved. Maria's mission was now to save her only grandson from being executed by a state that did not give a shit about him or her.

She wasn't naive to the fact that the district attorney and the police only called her when her son's killer was going to court, and lately they had been buzzing up her phone because her son's killer was granted a hearing by the Pennsylvania Superior Court because his trial attorney had failed to introduce his mental history records to the trial court. She felt disrespected that the only time they called her was when they needed her assistance to bury her grandson alive. The crookedness of the district attorney and the police department in Philadelphia lost its power to get her on their side, coming to signify demagoguery and arrogance, which left her with a bitter taste.

Lil' Bert could hear keys rattling, the door of the death row section on J-block swinging outward on parched hinges, and the footsteps of six COs and a lieutenant named Jackski, a fat, sloppy cracker with shitty breath.

"Ruiz, you have a visit! Prepare for your visit now!" Lieutenant Jackski yelled.

Lil' Bert knew the drill. He stripped naked and stood in front of his cell door with a ferocious hard-on.

"Oh, you think you're funny? Let's see how funny it will be when I cancel your visit, asshole!" Lieutenant Jackski said.

"I haven't violated any rules, have I? I did not know it was illegal to have a hard-on. I just woke up. You know how it is when a condemned man wakes up with a desperate hard-on."

"Hey, asshole! Do you want your visit or not?"

"What you think, Mr. Officer?" Lil' Bert replied as he stood buck naked, waiting for the lieutenant to dish out the orders.

"Okay, asshole, open your mouth, lift your tongue up, wiggle it around, rub your hands through your hair, pull your ears down, lift your nut sack up, dick, pull back the skin, turn around, bend over, spread your cheeks!

Asshole, I said spread 'em! I want to see your heartbeat. Lift your right foot up, wiggle your toes, lift your left foot up, and wiggle your toes. Okay, now get dressed!" Lieutenant Jackski instructed with a smile.

When Lil' Bert was handcuffed and shackled, he was led out of his cell and down a long, dark hallway where three other COs waited in a small room that had been designated as the visiting room for the capital cases.

Once he was seated in a secure booth, an old, well-kept woman approached the screen with a concerned smile. "Alberto!"

"Yes."

"I'm your grandmother. I'm happy to be here."

"I remember you from court."

A long silence let Lil' Bert know what she thought of him. Finally, Maria lifted her head up and locked eyes with him. If the screen were not separating them, she would have reached over and hugged him. Her eyes took a slow tour around the visiting room, and for a second she felt a sharp pain in her heart. "Son, this may sound strange to you, but I forgave you a long time ago. I am not here to judge you or to talk about your father. What's done is done. We cannot turn the clock back, so you must forgive yourself. I am here because I want to help you. I know the courts fucked you around. I know your lawyer sold you out. I know this because the district attorney consulted with me about sending you to death row. I want to help you. I want to bring you home with me where you belong." Maria could not overlook the fact that her grandson looked just like his father.

"Maria . . . Grandma . . . I'm not sure what you want me to call you. I have a few questions about my father. I know you said you are not here to speak of him, but I need answers. I need to know why he abandoned me. Why?" Lil' Bert was thirsty for answers.

"Son, your father didn't abandon you. He never knew you existed until your mother came around one day harassing him for money, claiming she was pregnant with you. Son, at that time, your father was a beat cop, and your mother was a hooker in North Philly. So when she came around, no one believed her, not me, not your father. About three years before his death, your father searched for you and your mother endlessly, but he could not find you because he never knew your name. He searched for your mother, but with only a street name he had no luck. There was not a day that passed he did not think of you. He loved you with all his heart. When your sister OD'd, he really went out of his way to look for you, even though he was a homicide detective. He made it his business to travel to North Philly every day to see if he could locate your mother." Maria's eyes became watery as she stared into Lil' Bert's eyes.

"I'm sorry I killed him. I didn't know it was him. What a way to meet a father for the first time, huh?"

"It's not your fault. You did what you had to do to survive the streets of Philly. I miss my only son, but things happen for a reason. God took him but gave me you. So now I must do what I have to do to help you out. Your father would want me to."

Maria felt an old paralysis. She sorted through her vocabulary for the right words, and her eyes dimmed slowly as the incandescence in a light bulb after the power goes out. Finally, she spoke again. "It's important for me to help you get out of here."

"Why?"

"Because you are the only bloodline I have left, that's why."

"How can you be so sure I'm your grandson?"

"We can have a DNA test done if that would make you feel better," she replied with a smile.

"Nah, I have no reason to doubt you. If you say you're my grandma, then you're my grandma. It feels good to have a grandma."

"I guess so, and it feels good to have a grandson," Maria replied. "Do you know you are half Puerto Rican and half Colombian?"

"No, I didn't know," Lil' Bert said, then added, "Where do we go from here?"

"I thought you'd never ask. However, I'll be up front with you, son. We're in this together. I'm the only person you have out here, so if you want me to help you out, the first thing you have to do is stop calling me Grandma and just call me Ma or Maria. 'Grandma' makes me feel old. Second, from this day on, I'll handle all your attorney fees. These court-appointed lawyers cannot and will not help you. And third, do not ever bullshit me or lie to me. When I ask you something, give it to me straight and raw. Believe me, I have seen more drama than you could imagine. Do not let this little old lady fool you! If anybody can help you, it's me. Am I getting beside myself?" Maria asked Lil' Bert, who was staring at his grandmother in disbelief. At that moment, he knew she was not a dummy.

"No, you're not getting beside yourself. I just never expected you to come off in that fashion."

"Listen here, son. Your father was law and order, and I'm proud of what he did with his life. Nevertheless, I came from a family of hustlers. Your great uncle, my brother, is the biggest heroin dealer in the city. If it's being sold in the city, it probably came through his hands. Your father never knew because my brother distanced himself from your father when he decided to become a cop, but we remain close, and he is prepared to use all his influence to help you out of here. You have a family who loves you.

"Now it's my understanding that you will be heading back to court next month. Your uncle has hired one of the best attorneys in the country to represent you. His name is Frank Wolfman, and he will be here to see you in a few days. I also understand your little girlfriend took off with your money and framed you up for two more murders. That could become a problem, but it's nothing we can't fix."

"How you know about this?" Lil' Bert asked her.

"I know a lot of things. My sources keep me well-informed," Maria replied, being careful she didn't tell him too much about how seriously she was involved in the game. It would ruin the mystique. She studied Lil' Bert's face and then raised her brow. "Have you ever heard of Nice-town Shareef? The North-side Don?"

Lil' Bert nodded. "Yes," he said, then added, "He's my old head. He always treated me like a son. Why do you ask?" He started to feel uneasy. Was his grandmother getting ready to drop another load on him and tell him that Nice-town Shareef was related to him? All of a sudden, for the first time in the conversation, he began to respect his grandmother's G-code. Although she was 64 years old, she was street buff to her core, and there was no doubt she meant business when she said she wanted to help him get off death row.

"Shareef is a great friend of my family, and he's willing to play his part on your behalf. He has some evidence that would rearrange the city's political structure, evidence that would threaten the prosecution's case against you."

Maria wasn't quite done speaking when Lieutenant Jackski appeared at her side and yelled to the roomful of people, "Ladies and gentlemen, visiting hours are now over! All visitors, please leave your visiting booths!"

Maria looked directly at Lil' Bert's eyes and held her hand up to the screen and said, "I love you, *hihoito,* son!

I'll be back soon, but expect a visit from the lawyer soon. Call me tonight if you can."

"Ladies and gentlemen, visiting hours are now over! All inmates must back away from their assigned visiting booths now! Refusing to do so will be considered refusing to obey a direct order, and a misconduct will be awarded!" Jackski yelled angrily.

After going through the same humiliating process of stripping naked and exposing his nakedness to some faggot-ass COs, Lil' Bert was escorted back to his cell.

That night as he lay in his bunk, he could see himself back on the block doing what he did best: raining terror on all those weak-ass niggas who wished for his fall. For the first time in a year, he actually believed he could get out of prison. If his grandmother was who she claimed she was, there was no doubt he would be back on the block soon.

He closed his eyes and drifted off to la-la land.

Chapter Twenty-seven

It's Your Call

The plan was a simple one. Maria Vasquez Ruiz was scheduled to meet with the district attorney to discuss Lil' Bert's upcoming hearing. The meeting was to take place in Roger Dean's private office, where they weren't likely to be interrupted. She would bring Nice-town Shareef along with her to ensure the deal got sealed.

"Think he'll go for it?" Maria asked Shareef as they sat in the living room, viewing the freshly inherited DVD of Roger Dean in the middle of a fuck-fest with murder victim Reverend Cruz and homo thug Bolo.

"That greasy motherfucker has no choice. If he acts like he wants to play games, every reporter and every media outlet in the city will receive a copy by noon tomorrow. With people like Roger Dean, you must be ready to give it to him dirty and raw. Let me handle this."

"I trust you with my life. I have no doubt you won't do anything less than handle your business. Are you ready to do this?"

"Yeah, let's roll!" Shareef said, certain that he would not only gain Lil' Bert's freedom, but also freedom for his brother, Ali, who was serving a life sentence for a drug-related murder.

Once they arrived at the district attorney's office in downtown Philadelphia, Shareef carefully placed the copy of the DVD in the inside of his dark Sean John suit. He grabbed Maria's hand and made his entrance into the DA's office. After passing the security checkpoint, they took the elevator to the tenth floor, where Roger Dean waited behind a brown desk with two chairs in front of it.

When Dean saw Maria and Shareef enter his office, he put on his game face, the one he used to convince victims' families that he was concerned about them when in fact he wasn't. "Good afternoon, Mrs. Ruiz! Good to see you could make it today!" he said, extending his hand to her.

"Good to see you too, Mr. Dean. Oh, this here is my friend, Shareef. He's here to help me understand the legal process of this stressful situation and, of course, for moral support as well," Maria stated, locking eyes with Dean.

"Good to have you here, sir!" Roger said, extending his hand to Shareef. *I've seen this man before. I can't remember where, but he sure looks familiar,* Roger thought as he proceeded to sit down behind his desk.

"Mrs. Ruiz, your son's killer is embarking on a new legal battle that may produce some satisfying results for any death-row inmate. My office is prepared to fight this scumbag until he is put to death, as the jury demanded. Nevertheless, it will be a long process. Your son's killer is claiming that his trial attorney violated his constitutional rights when she failed to introduce his mental history medical records to the trial judge. It will be in the interest of the Commonwealth to have you and all your son's supporters present at the hearing." Roger Dean knew victims' survivors always looked forward to stick it to the offender every chance they got, so he expected nothing less from Maria Vasquez Ruiz.

"Mr. Dean, I don't believe I can assist you or your office in this case any longer. There is nothing in the world that will bring back my son. I've already lost my only son, and

I'm not about to lose my grandson to the system," Maria stated firmly.

"Mrs. Ruiz, I'm confused. What do you mean by your 'grandson'? The prosecution is not aware of the accused being related to you." Dean was now sweating heavily.

"Mr. Dean, if I may butt in, we can handle this situation like grown folks or we can take this public. I'm hoping you consider our request and withdraw all the charges against Alberto 'Lil' Bert' Ruiz on his next court hearing, and we can all move on. If not, you can start writing the eulogy for your political career," Shareef said with a sly smile.

"I'm not sure of what I'm hearing, but if I'm correct, I believe blackmailing an official of the court is a punishable crime that carries a prison penalty." Roger Dean felt sure he was having an impact on Mrs. Ruiz and Shareef. But Shareef's facial expression spoke otherwise.

"No, Mr. Dean, this is not blackmail. It's more of a trade-off, a fair exchange," Shareef replied while handing the DVD to him. Then he added, "If I were you, I would view this DVD, and then we can discuss our trade-off."

Roger Dean was hesitant at first to grab the DVD, but his curiosity got the best of him, and he snatched it out of Shareef's hand. He inserted it into the TV set in his office. After a few seconds of him playing with the remote control, the images popped up on the screen. His eyes widened when he saw himself engaged in a threesome with murder victims Reverend Cruz and Bolo. His heart wanted to burst out of his chest.

"I'm sorry to disappoint you, Mr. Dean, but this is not personal. It's business," Shareef said as he stared at Maria with a smile.

"Son of a bitch! You bastard you! You think you can come into my office and wave this shit in my face? I'm not moved by this, you bastard!" Roger Dean was losing his cool. His taste buds were becoming sour, and he felt like he was choking on his own saliva. "Nobody would ever believe you for Christ's sake!"

"Oh, yes, they will! I promise you this, sir. If I don't walk out of this office with a deal, CNN, ABC, CBS, C-SPAN, and every judge in this city will have a copy of your porn tape. What would it look like to have the city's district attorney in a porn tape with two murder victims? And to top it off, he prosecuted the prime suspect for a cop killing. That shit would look real ugly for you, my man. I'm sure you don't want to sit on your ass and wait for the shit to hit the fan, do you?" Shareef knew he was in charge of the situation.

Roger Dean hesitated, forgetting what he was going to say. Inflamed by the boldness of Shareef, he wasn't quite ready to throw in the towel, not when he knew he had an entire legal system pledging its services to whomever he wanted to prosecute. Never did he think that one day he would have to betray his oath because of his sexual adventures. Thus, unhampered by the watchdogs of justice, he wasn't ready to give up his lifestyle, and damned if he was going to let a scorned affair destroy his life.

Sensitive to the pressure Shareef was applying, not to mention the scrutiny of whoever else might get their hands on the DVD, he folded like the faggot he was. "How can we get rid of this mess? Who else knows about this DVD?"

"No one else . . . yet! If we can come to an understanding, no one will ever know about it. My word is bond!" Shareef said, winking at Maria, who was sitting in a chair enjoying the show.

"What are we talking about?" Roger Dean wanted to know exactly the terms of the trade-off.

"Alberto 'Lil' Bert' Ruiz has a hearing next month. Make the charges go away. You know what you have to do. Work your magic, Mr. DA. I also want time cut for my little brother, Ali Jones. He is serving a life sentence in Graterford Prison. You prosecuted him. Remember the Tenth Street firebombing? He already served eleven years." Shareef was firm in his demand.

"What? Are you crazy? I can't cut a cop killer loose! The city will go berserk!"

"Sure you can! You're the DA! You're the man! It's your call to determine who goes to jail and who don't. Pin the case on someone else. I don't give a fuck who! Bert walks, and my brother gets time served. It's your call." Shareef was now standing up, his eyes following Roger Dean, who was staring out the window.

Dean's face wore an expression of someone who would rather be anyplace else, which was close to the truth. For someone who made a living out of putting criminals away for life, this moment was exposing all his weaknesses. "How do I know all this won't appear again after I handle my part of the trade-off?" he asked, trying to get some kind of reassurance that this drama would be put behind him.

"It won't. Once my brother and Lil' Bert are out of prison, you or anyone in this city will never ever hear from us again. And the only original copy of your porn tape will be handed to you personally. I understand it's unethical for an officer of the court to make side deals with criminals, but in this case, consider it a career investment," Shareef said, hovering behind Roger Dean.

"I would need some time to think about this offer. I do have the right to think things over, don't I?"

"Yes, you do, but time is of the essence. You have until Lil' Bert's next court appearance. After that, shit will hit the fan!" Shareef stated firmly, grabbing Maria's hand and walking out of the district attorney's office feeling sure of himself.

"Do you think he's going to bend on this?" Maria asked as they rode the elevator back down to the first floor.

"Yes. He's already bent over. He's just trying to buy some time to see if we're going to back down. This situation is inconvenient for him. He would make arrangements to demoralize the justice system to save his ass. Patience, ma!" Shareef felt like he conquered the world.

Two weeks after his encounter with Maria Vasquez Ruiz and Shareef, District Attorney Roger Dean was prepared to lay out his fact-finding and new developments in the most sensational murder trial in Philadelphia's recent history. As the chief district attorney, he had the power to build or destroy any case he wanted. In this case, he was backed into a corner, so he assembled his most trusted assistant district attorneys and called for a closed-door private meeting with the trial judge, Tommy Sebo.

Dressed in a black double-breasted suit with a yellow handkerchief in three points in the pocket, Roger Dean looked as if he was ready to put on one of his many theatrical performances. Only this time, his career depended on it. He kept his hands folded in front of him and said nothing.

Judge Sebo took a seat behind his desk and instructed Mr. Dean to begin.

"Your Honor, I'm sorry I have to bother you on such short notice. But it has come to the attention of the district attorney's office, through our investigators, that we may have the wrong man sitting on death row for the murder of Detective Alberto Ruiz."

As Roger Dean spoke, Judge Sebo's eyebrows raised straight up.

"So, Your Honor, in the interest of justice, my office is prepared to withdraw all the charges against the defendant, Alberto 'Lil' Bert' Ruiz. By the end of the day, I will have my assistant hand deliver the motion to withdraw charges."

"Mr. Dean, how can you be so sure that the wrong man has been charged and convicted?"

"Your Honor, we have every reason to believe that the defendant in question is innocent. We have a suspect already serving time, the actual murder weapon, and a signed confession. The suspect is a twenty-five-year-old black male by the name of Ron Dupree, with a rap sheet as long as a football field. His signed confession was taken three weeks after our defendant in question was arrested, but homicide detectives dismissed his claim as absurd because of the suspect we had in custody. But through our informants, we learned that the suspect has been talking about killing a cop. After an internal investigation and ballistics tests on the murder weapon we recovered from the suspect's girlfriend, we came to the conclusion that the wrong man has been convicted." Roger Dean, for a moment, believed the bullshit he was feeding Judge Sebo.

"Mr. Dean, I will take this new information into consideration, and after I review your motion and new evidence, I will render my decision at the next scheduled hearing, which is May twenty-eighth. However, Mr. Dean, off the record, why go through the motion of embarrassing this court, your office, and basically the city police department by cutting an accused cop killer loose when we could just keep his ass on death row?"

"Your Honor, since we're talking off the record, I will take the liberty to express my reasons why. Justice is meant to be served correctly. This case can backfire on us if we decided to overlook the facts. Any good attorney

will have a field day with this new information, so why
not beat them to the starting line and do it ourselves?
That way, we keep the integrity of the court unquestionable. The bastard is probably going to end up back in the
system anyway."

Judge Sebo understood where Mr. Dean was coming
from. "I guess we can let the bad guys win one." He hated
to reverse a jury's verdict. In his thirty-two years on the
bench, he never reversed a conviction, even when he
knew the prosecution had tampered with the case. In his
eyes, putting niggers and spics behind bars was his civic
duty. If they were in front of his bench, they were guilty
of something. He enjoyed the fear the defendants always
displayed when he served them their sentences and
cracked his gavel. But this case was different. The murder
victim was a decorated police officer, and the defendant
was a coldhearted street thug who showed the court no
respect, even refusing to stand when his death sentence
was handed down to him. *If I grant the district attorney's motion, every other nigger or spic who sets foot in
my courtroom will have to pay the price!* he thought as
he watched Roger Dean walk out of his private office.

Chapter Twenty-eight

The Dirty South

The last two weeks had been nothing but a state of madness for Shareef and Maria, so Shareef decided to treat himself to a little vacation down in Atlanta. It was his home away from Philly. In Philly, he was the Don, the nigga everybody wanted to be. But in the ATL, he was just a black man who enjoyed going shopping at the Lennox Mall's most expensive shops.

ATL also offered him the chance to be exposed to the way hardworking Black folks lived. The privileged and the poor in Atlanta took pride in their culture, whereas in Philly, the living conditions were insane. Motherfuckers only cared about money, bitches, and pussy. Niggas couldn't see past the game. So when he visited the ATL last year, he instantly felt at home, dropping $250,000 on a condo, which he used to get away from the bullshit in Philly.

Shareef was at the local bank, filling out a money order for his little brother. It was a weekly endeavor that Shareef had been doing since Ali got locked up. He could have sent him a big chunk of money, but he thought it better to send it weekly to give Ali something to look forward to each week, keep his spirits up.

Damn! I can't wait 'til my little brother touches the streets again! I'ma show him what life is all about. I miss my little nigga! Throughout his whole bid, he never complained about being locked down for shit he didn't do. He just held his head up high and took the case like a man. When the judge smacked him with a life bid, he smiled and told the judge to kiss his ass, then turned around and knocked his lawyer the fuck out right in the courtroom. The shit was hilarious, because Roger Dean ran out of the courtroom screaming like a little bitch. Now he must provide to my brother the justice he's been denying niggas for years.

When Ali got locked up, Shareef wasn't quite the major player he was today. He never got to experience or see the work Shareef had to put in to move up the ranks in the game. He had heard the stories niggas told in the penitentiary, and he saw plenty of pictures of Shareef flashing wads of cash in front of new cars, but none of that shit mattered to him if he couldn't be home to celebrate with his big brother.

Shareef hadn't dropped the bomb on him about the possibility of him coming home soon because he didn't want to give a nigga hope unless he was sure his plan was going to come through with no problem. The last thing his brother needed was some false dreams. Dreams are all penitentiary niggas talk about, so he wasn't going to tell Ali he was coming home until he was sure. *I might as well drop this nigga a kite,* Shareef thought as he was getting ready to seal the envelope with the money order.

What's popping, my dude?
Yo! I take this time to drop you a few lines. I know you probably don't want to be bothered with me telling you about what's going on out here. Nevertheless, here is some change for commissary. Hopefully, soon you will be home. They can't keep a real nigga like you down for long.

I will be up to see you next week, so be on point.
You know how those nasty-ass guards like to keep a
nigga waiting. You know our motto. "Fuck dream-
ing! Dreaming is for suckas! It's about taking what
you want in life!" Never forget that!
    Be safe and strong.
    Blood in, blood out.
    Your Brotha,
    The Don
    P.S. Spread the love around to all the real niggas
in there.

Just when Shareef finished sealing the envelope, his
cell phone went off. He looked at it, and it was his private
line, which only a few people had access to. He didn't feel
like answering it, but when he looked at the number, he
knew something was up, so he dialed Maria's number
back. She answered it on the first ring.

"What's up, ma?"

"Did you handle our business yet?"

"Not yet. It will be handled today."

"I want her to suffer the same way my grandson is
suffering over her dirty ass."

Shareef smiled to himself because Maria was a grimy
old motherfucker. Although she had the appearance of a
fragile old lady, she had the heart of a killer, and it didn't
hurt that she had the bankroll to back up her shit. If she
were younger, he probably would've laid some serious
pipe down on her. Who knew? If she kept spoiling him
the way she had been doing, keeping his supply of heroin
stacked, he might go against his principals and twist her
old pussy up just one time. He saw the way she'd been
looking at him when they were together. Although she
always proclaimed to love him like a son, Shareef knew
better. He knew if he really wanted, Maria would let him

tap that ass. For 64 years old, Maria looked every little
bit of 50, a good 50. She dressed well, kept in good shape,
and her sophisticated mannerisms made her attractive.
"I hear you, ma. I'll give you a call when all is done. I'll
see you in two days." He clicked his phone off before she
could say another word. She was long-winded, and he
didn't feel like holding a long conversation on his private
line.

He lay back and waited for a call from Gorilla, a reliable
hit man from West Baltimore who was in the ATL for the
sole purpose of delivering a message to MaryLuz.

Since arriving in the ATL, MaryLuz had been reinvent-
ing herself, creating a lucrative catering business that
serviced the upper class. In a little over ten months since
she double-crossed Lil' Bert and took off to the ATL with
her then 8-month-old son and $300,000 of Bert's money,
she had been living large.

Her new man, Rondall, was an executive with the
Atlanta Hawks, making Philly's Catering Service,
MaryLuz's joint, the exclusive party planners for all the
ballers in the Atlanta Hawks' club. Her days of running
with drug dealers were over. She was now a mother and
wife, enjoying a lavish lifestyle.

She thought of Lil' Bert once in a while, but not often,
and she wondered if he was hating himself for being so
fucking stupid in trusting her with his cash, even after he
had beaten her ass in public over some bullshit. A little
tiny scar on the right side of her face reminded her of the
ass kicking he had put on her. *That nigga got what he
deserved! I pray they fry his ass straight to hell! Stupid-
ass nigga really thought I was going to ride his bid out
with him. Sorry-ass nigga should just be executed for
being stupid. But then again, most niggas in prison*

believe they're slick and always want some ho to ride with them when they're down, even after they dogged them when they were out on the streets. Fuck him! He could charge his loss to the game.

MaryLuz's thoughts were interrupted when she heard the bell ringing on the door of her Philly's Catering Services in downtown Atlanta. At first she thought it was Ito, her son, playing around, but the well-dressed, light-skinned brother standing at the door brought her to her feet. Gorilla was the first of her many appointments for the day. *This must be the one throwing the album-release party for Luda,* she thought as she buzzed him in. "Good afternoon, sir," she said as she extended her hand to Gorilla with a warm smile.

"It's a pleasure to meet you. I heard a lot about you and your services," Gorilla said, scoping out the place.

"I pride myself in providing the best catering services in town."

"That's why I'm here. I'm not looking for anything too fancy. This event is an album-release party. A lot of industry heads will be attending. I'm expecting anywhere from six to seven hundred people, so I want the Philly Special: finger food, plenty of cheesesteaks, and whatever else the Philly Special brings. I'll be paying in cash." Gorilla reached into his Gucci bag and pulled out a wad of bills. "How much is the bill?"

MaryLuz pulled out a calculator. "Let's split the difference and say six hundred fifty people at seventy-five dollars per person." She typed in the numbers. "$48,750. I can give you a ten percent discount on that. Will you be needing alcohol as well?"

"Yes, open bar."

"Great." MaryLuz got up from her desk and went to grab Ito, who was trying to reach for a bottle of soda that was sitting on top of a glass table.

As soon as MaryLuz grabbed Ito, Gorilla put his pistol to her face and covered her mouth. "Bitch, if you scream, you die! Now where do you keep the money?"

"I don't keep money in here!" MaryLuz replied. She was scared to death. Her body began trembling when she felt Gorilla's dick stiffen against her fat ass.

Gorilla moved MaryLuz and her son into the back room, which served as a kitchen to Philly's Catering Service, and taped her wrists behind her back, then did the same to Ito, who was screaming at the top of his lungs. Since Gorilla couldn't take the chance of having anyone hear his crying, he slapped some duct tape over his small lips, closing his mouth.

"Bitch, we can make this easy, or we can turn it into something ugly. Now bend your fat ass over that table!" Gorilla wasn't into taking pussy, but this was business. It was part of the contract. *Business is business. It's never personal,* he thought as he pulled MaryLuz's dress up over her back, pulled her thong string to the side, and exposed her asshole.

MaryLuz almost fainted when she felt Gorilla's huge dick rubbing against her luscious asshole. "Please don't do this in front of my son! I'm all he's got!"

"You dirty-ass whore! Shorty doesn't deserve a whore like you for a mother! He'll probably turn out to be as trifling as you! I got something for his ass too!" Gorilla's eyes rolled to the back of his head as he made contact with MaryLuz's asshole. "Damn, this mothafucka feels good!" He spit in the palm of his hand.

"Please don't do this! Please don't!" MaryLuz pleaded, but her pleas weren't heard.

Without any warning, Gorilla rammed his huge dick into her asshole. MaryLuz passed out for a few seconds, but the muffled sound of her son kept her awake while Gorilla humiliated her in front of him and busted her ass open until she couldn't take it anymore and shit on his dick. She would have preferred to die, but the look on her son's face told her he needed her.

Once Gorilla pulled his shitty dick out of her, MaryLuz tried to force a scream out of her mouth, but she couldn't because her mouth was stuffed with the barrel of his gun.

Gorilla pulled his gun out of her mouth and duct-taped it. He then ordered her to lie on the floor. "Bitch, I'm just getting started. You haven't seen shit yet. There is a price to pay for breaking the playa's code. I know you ain't think you could just double-cross a nigga and get away with it. It's time to pay up!"

He was expressing a level of hatred MaryLuz had never seen in a human being. She watched helplessly as he cleaned himself up with some of her Philly's Catering Service fancy napkins. Afterward, he stuffed the napkins into his Gucci bag. He was careful not to leave any evidence of ever being there.

Gorilla was feeling himself, so he poured half a bottle of cooking oil into a pot on the stove and let it boil.

"Please don't hurt my son!" MaryLuz tried to say through the duct tape.

"Bitch, I can't hear you!" Gorilla replied as he gripped little Ito by his feet and held him up in the air.

MaryLuz was trembling violently, attempting to protect her son from what she knew was imminent.

"You see, bitch, this game has no rules. Your trifling ass needs to learn how to respect a nigga's G-code," Gorilla said.

MaryLuz tried to reach into the depth of her core to turn herself loose, but she couldn't.

"Bitch, this is a personal message from a lost friend," Gorilla said as he pulled out a photo of Lil' Bert and held it to her face. Then he grabbed a turkey baster and filled it with the boiling oil he had on the stove. He bent MaryLuz over the table again and jammed the baster full of hot oil up her ass. The burning sensation immediately made her pass out. He was making sure that no trace of his semen was left. The oil burned MaryLuz's asshole into eternity.

"Tell God I said hi, you nasty ho!" he said as he placed his gun between her eyes and squeezed the trigger six times. Nobody heard anything because of the silencer on his gun. The bullets pierced through her brain, lodging into the floor where her limp body lay.

Gorilla put Lil' Bert's photo back into his pocket, picked up his Gucci bag, and walked out of Philly's Catering Service as if nothing ever happened.

The macabre scene inside of Philly's Catering Services looked like another robbery gone bad. These kinds of cases didn't get solved. They became stories for *America's Most Wanted* and other TV crime shows.

Once Gorilla was en route back to West Baltimore, he dialed the number he was told to dial once the job was done. Shareef picked up on the second ring.

"Job done!" was all Gorilla said into the receiver like a true professional.

Shareef wasn't interested in details. All he wanted to know was that the job was done. Immediately after receiving that phone call, he decided to cut his vacation short. He wanted to be out of the city before the news of MaryLuz's death broke. His only concern was that the police found the body in time to at least save her baby son.

He was oblivious to the fact that the hit man his connect in B'More put on the job never left witnesses. A child was considered a witness, so he had to go. One of the reasons the Murdering Squad never revealed the identity of their hit men was because most of them fulfilled hits in the most brutal way.

Back in Philly, the news of MaryLuz hit the streets like a tornado. When Shareef saw it on CNN, his heart was broken, not because of MaryLuz, but because her child was not supposed to be part of the game. He called the connect in charge of the Murdering Squad in Baltimore, and all they could tell him was, "What difference does it make? The job got done!"

Shareef blamed himself for not giving instructions to the connect when he put out the hit. He vowed to look and search for the hit man who carried out the hit and torture his ass after he handled all his business in Philly.

Two days later, he received a FedEx package with all the information he had forwarded to the connect in B'More, which were pictures of MaryLuz, her business address, and the picture of Lil' Bert.

Killing kids was not part of my plan. Forgive me, God! he thought as he prepared to visit his brother in prison, hopefully for the last time.

Chapter Twenty-nine

Boo-ya, Trick!

Nice-town Shareef sat in his car at Graterford Prison, looking up at the forty-five-foot wall that was decorated with barbed wire circles at the top and surveillance cameras every fifty feet. *Now who the fuck is gonna climb that wall? A nigga got to be a bad mothafucka to even think about it,* he thought as he watched a couple of nasty-looking, torn-up, hating-ass, fake-hair-wearing female COs standing by the front gate. They were hating on some fly-ass Puerto Rican chick who was shaking her ass like she was crazy.

For the past eleven years, Shareef had visited Graterford Prison every other week, so he saw his share of prison vixens getting it on right in the parking lot with other bitches over a nigga on lockdown. Sometimes the drama would be caused by the nasty whore COs who would purposely call two bitches at the same time to visit the same person.

The rationalization of where his brother had been for the last decade finally hit him. Even though he tried, he couldn't even begin to understand what it was like to spend a day on lockdown and feeling less than a man. *Damn! This is where half of my niggas are in for life! This is the infamous G-Ford where real niggas do their time.*

Shareef snapped out of his daydream when he spotted Maria's car pulling up next to his. He stepped out of his car and embraced her, and together they walked to the visitor's entrance. Once they were processed, Maria was told to wait for an escort who would pick her up in a prison van and drive her around to the back of the prison, which was where the capital-case visiting room was located.

Meanwhile, Shareef had endured the humiliation of being told to walk through a metal detector, which kept going off every time he stepped through it.

"Sir, try again! Do you have any metal on you? Anything that can set the machine off?"

This bitch either is stupid or has some severe mental problems asking me some dumb shit like that! Shareef thought as he again searched his pockets to make sure he was clean. Again he attempted to go through the metal detector, but it kept going off.

By now, two hillbilly asshole male guards approached him as if they were real fucking cops. "Sir, you have two choices. You can either allow us to strip search you, or you can have a screen visit. But for now, you must step aside so the other visitors can go through," one of the male guards said, mean mugging Shareef as if he suspected him of something.

"My man, what are you implying? I don't come here to be harassed by you phony-ass COs. I come here to visit my people. In fact, I want to speak to a lieutenant or a captain, 'cause I don't have shit on me." Just when Shareef was about to snap on the CO who was mean mugging him, the metal detector went off, drawing everyone's attention.

"Bitch, I am not the one you want to fuck with today! I been through this machine four times!" a thick-ass, around-the-way chick hollered at the nasty-looking guard who was behind the desk enjoying the look of distress on the faces of the people when she denied them access to visit their loved ones.

Just then, a more level-headed guard appeared at the front desk and checked the metal detector, realizing that the machine was turned on high, beyond its normal capacity, which automatically made it go off when anyone walked through. The crowd of people cheered the CO, because now they could finally get into the visiting room to see their loved ones.

The CO at the front desk knew what was wrong with the metal detector all along, but she refused to fix it because she was hating on all the chicks who wanted to come into the institution to visit their men. On the other hand, the male CO who came to the rescue only fixed it because he was trying to flirt with one of the visitors who was wearing a skintight body suit that was choking her pussy to death.

The female CO at the front desk waved for Shareef to step to the front of the line, but he refused and continued to step to the back of the line. "I'm good!" he said as he patiently waited his turn. When he reached the front desk again, the female CO tried to make friendly talk with him, but he ignored the shit out of her. *I don't need any favors from this torn-up ho,* he thought as he went through the metal detector with no problem.

When he made it to the visiting room, Ali was already waiting. "Damn, bro! What took you so long?" Ali asked with a smile, trying to break the tension his big brother was feeling.

"Those clowns up there tried to play me hard. I almost lost it!" Shareef said as he embraced his brother with a tight hug. "Yo, let's go talk out in the yard."

They stepped out to the visiting yard, where kids ran around while their parents tried to blindside the guard and get their freak on. Desperate people do desperate things, and some females get off on visiting niggas in prison with the sole purpose of getting their pussy torn up in public.

After twenty minutes of walking the yard, Ali and Shareef stopped in front of a picnic table where a young couple sat feeling each other up. The young prisoner took it as an opportunity to get himself a shot of pussy, as he instructed his girl to sit on his lap, which she gladly did. With Ali and Shareef blocking the guards' view, the young girl rode her man's lap as if she were riding a horse.

"You see that shit, bro? That kind of shit is nasty, but I can't hate, because man wasn't meant to live without the affection of a woman."

The chick who was riding her man overheard Shareef and smiled.

"Man, not everyone in here is lucky like that. I'd rather be in that position than go back to my cell and beat off on some video chick, dig me? Some of these chicks who come up here are nasty as hell, but they get much love, 'cause they keep a nigga in here stress free. That's the role of a prison vixen." Ali wasn't about to hate on a nigga for getting some pussy. *It is what it is. A nigga got to do what he got to do to stay on his hustle.*

"Bro, listen here. You been in this place too long, but that shit is about to change. Your time in this place is getting short. Soon you will be swinging in some exclusive pussy, believe me. Don't ask me no questions. Just listen carefully. In thirty days, you will be going back to court, and a plea deal will be offered to you for time served. The DA wants the conviction. At the hearing, a lawyer by the name of Sylvester Rabinowitz will be representing you. Take the deal and walk out of this place a free man!" Shareef said with a serious face.

"Man, how you gonna get this life bid off my back?" Ali shook his head, hoping to get his brother to at least give him a hint of what he was planning.

"Put it this way—some things are not to be spoken about. Opportunities like this come once in a lifetime. Are you prepared for them? I told you not to ask me any questions, because I don't want to lie to you. When they come pick you up for court, kiss this place goodbye!"

For a minute Shareef looked around the yard and felt somehow connected. Part of his life had become accustomed to the bullshit he'd been through in the past eleven years while visiting Ali. No one really knew what it was like to have a loved one on lockdown until they experienced it first-hand. Shareef had experienced it in the rawest way, and now it was time to move on. His loyalty toward his brother and the game was unquestionable. He hugged his brother and walked out of Graterford Prison on cloud nine.

Down in the death-row visiting room, Maria waited patiently for the guards to escort Bert down to his visit. It seemed like every week it took longer and longer for them to bring him down. Although she had become a familiar face, occasionally some arrogant asshole guard would run his mouth and blare out some dumb shit toward her. *Hopefully this will be over soon,* she thought, smiling when she saw Lil' Bert appear on the other side of the screen.

"Hey! How are you?"

"I'm still alive."

"What took them so long to bring you down here?"

"One of the guys got his death warrant signed two days ago and decided he wanted to go out like a soldier, so he sliced a section guard's face open from ear to ear with a razor blade through the cell bars. And before the goon squad could get in his cell to beat his ass, the mothafucka hanged himself with his bedsheets. Ma, he fucked the guard's face up real bad! On top of that, he had AIDS!" Bert said with a smile, happy that the playing field was leveled.

Carlos had hanged himself, robbing the State of his death, but at the same time, he passed a death sentence on to the guard, because the razor he used to slice his face open was infected with his death sentence, AIDS.

"Well, I'm glad you're safe," Maria said. "So did the lawyer come to visit you yet?"

"Yes. He came up yesterday and informed me that things are looking good for me. He looked like a good lawyer, but I don't have any faith in the legal system. So whatever happens, happens. No matter what, I'ma still be me," Bert replied, not getting his hopes up for any court appearance. He was just happy to be able to get out of his cell for a few hours and see the city.

"Did you see the news of your little girlfriend?"

"That bitch got what she deserved. Crossing a nigga while he's down. I'm just mad I wasn't the one who did it." To him, she didn't die a brutal death. He wanted to chop her ass up in pieces and flush her ass down the toilet.

Maria looked at her grandson and hoped for the day she could shower him with the motherly love he so much needed in his life. *Then he might not be so angry and murderous.* "So tell me. What is the first thing you want to do if you get out of here today?"

"If that happened, the first thing I'd want to do is take a good bath. Then I want to eat a good meal. After that, you know! I want to spend a week with some beautiful lady. That's what every man in here wishes for," Lil' Bert replied with a smile.

"Maybe we can make that happen for you. What you think?"

"Ma, if you can make this happen, I would kiss your feet for the rest of your life!"

Maria smiled. "You'd be surprised at what I could make happen! Nevertheless, if and when you get out of here, before we celebrate, we're going to the cemetery to visit your father's grave. It would really mean a lot to me if you personally asked him for forgiveness. Although he is dead, it would make me feel at peace knowing you at least visited his grave once. Is that too much to ask for?" she asked in a low whisper.

"Nah, that's not too much. I'll do it if you come with me."

Lil' Bert couldn't imagine that soon he would be a free man again. He had mastered the art of playing head games with Maria. He had no intention of ever living under her roof if he ever were released from prison. In the meantime, he was going to keep telling her what she wanted to hear. He enjoyed the fat money orders she sent him on a weekly basis, the visits she blessed him with, and on top of that, the lawyer she hired to represent him. What else could a nigga on death row wish for?

"Of course I will go with you! I would never leave your side, son!" Maria blared as a tear escaped her eye.

"Why are you crying?"

"Because I love you, and I want to see you enjoy your life. It hurts me every time I see you chained up like an animal. I want you to be happy."

Maria felt good knowing that her plan was unfolding with no interruptions. *It doesn't get any better than this!* she thought as she placed her hand on the screen like she always did before she left. "I'll see you in court. Have a little bit of faith, and don't worry about anything. I will protect you from all harm. Love you!" She pushed her chair back, got up, and followed the guard, who escorted her back to the prison van.

Out in the parking lot, she hopped into Shareef's car and discussed her future plans. "I really do have a soft spot in my heart for that boy. He's my blood," she expressed to Shareef as he stared at the guard who mean mugged him when he first arrived to visit.

"Did you tell him he's coming home?"

"No!"

"Why not?"

"Because I want it to be a surprise for him. If I tell him, the whole hood would know about it, and that could fuck our plans up. Let it be a surprise. Did you tell your brother?"

"Yeah, I had to. Trust me, he knows how to keep his lips sealed," Shareef said with a smile.

"Soon I will have a happy family again!" Maria paused, then busted out laughing. Shareef just nodded his head.

Maria opened the door to his car, looked over at Shareef, and winked at him. It was their sign of communication when one of their plans was taking on a life of its own, and this one was on its way to producing more than expected. She drove home in a state of excitement about her easy mark.

On April 1, Ali Jones was woken out of his sleep at 4:30 in the morning to be taken to court. After he was held for four hours in the receiving room of the jail, two sheriffs came to pick him up in an unmarked state police car.

Arriving at the Criminal Justice Center in downtown Philadelphia left Ali in disarray. It had been eleven years since he last saw the streets, and everything had changed, at least in his eyes. The cars, the people, the buildings, the city, even the air smelled better than the contaminated air he had been breathing in Graterford.

As soon as he was placed in the holding cell, a young lawyer by the name of Sylvester Rabinowitz came to the cell to explain to him what was taking place.

"Mr. Jones, my name is Sylvester Rabinowitz, and I want to explain to you what will be taking place today. The district attorney is filing a motion to have your sentence revoked and is offering you a deal of time served. If you agree to this deal, you could walk out of this building a free man, no strings attached. What do you want me to do?" The young lawyer already knew the answer from speaking with Shareef, but he had to play it safe and follow the court procedures as the attorney on file.

"What do I have to do?"

"Just enter a guilty plea when the judge asks you. It's as simple as that."

"Take the deal. Let's do this!"

"All right. They're coming to escort you to the courtroom in five minutes. See you in there," the young attorney said as the sheriff let him out of the cell.

Five minutes later, Ali stood in front of Commonwealth Judge Lisa A. Richards.

"Your Honor, ladies and gentlemen of the court, my name is Roger Dean, district attorney for the City of Philadelphia. In the interest of justice, my office is withdrawing the charges against the defendant. The case in question dates back eleven years, and since then, new evidence has come to light that minimizes the defendant's involvement. Therefore, we petition this court to accept my office's motion."

"Mr. Dean, it is my understanding that the defendant will be entering a guilty plea in exchange for time served. Is that correct?"

"Yes, Your Honor, that is correct. We believe that the defendant has served a significant amount of time, which satisfies the penalty he would have received." Roger Dean was playing his role to a T.

"Mr. Rabinowitz, do you want to address the court?"

"Yes, Your Honor."

"Go ahead."

"Your Honor, the defendant in this case is a thirty-one-year-old man who deeply regrets his involvement in the crime in question. However, in the past eleven years he has taken advantage of the great programs our correctional system has to offer. He is a prime example of redemption and rehabilitation. And if he's given a second chance, this court would not have to worry about seeing him ever again. Thank you, Your Honor." Rabinowitz was making sure that he earned his $10,000 retainer fee that he charged Shareef.

"Mr. Dean, if neither of the parties has anything else to present to the court, I would like to enter my ruling."

"No, Your Honor. I believe both parties share the same interests," Dean stated, trying not to delay the process.

"Mr. Jones, this court finds no reason to deny the district attorney's motion, so I will accept the offer they presented to you if you find it appropriate to accept. Have you spoken to your attorney about it?"

"Yes, Your Honor, I have."

"Do you understand the terms of the deal offered to you?"

"Yes, Your Honor, I do."

"So how do you plead to the charges of involuntary manslaughter?"

"I plead guilty, Your Honor."

"Let the record show that Mr. Jones pleads guilty to the charges of involuntary manslaughter. Therefore, the court sentences the defendant to the penalty of five to ten years in the Department of Corrections. Since the defendant has served eleven years in state custody, this court will consider time served already, and the defendant is hereby ordered to be released from custody immediately.

Good luck in your new start at life, Mr. Jones." The crack-
ing of the judge's gavel brought the courtroom to its feet.

Shareef smiled at his brother and reached over the table where he sat in disbelief. "You know our motto. 'Fuck
dreaming! Dreaming is for suckas! It's about taking what
you want in life!' Never forget that! I'll be waiting for you
in the front. It'll probably take about a half hour for them
to process the paperwork. Love you, my little nigga!" he
said as the two sheriffs escorted Ali to the holding cell
until his paperwork got processed.

Alberto Ruiz, better known as Lil' Bert, sat quietly in
the same courtroom where he was sentenced to death,
surrounded by his new army of lawyers.

Frank Wolfman and his team were ready to expose
the corrupt justice system to its core. To him, nobody
could place Lil' Bert at the scene of the crime at the time
Detective Ruiz was killed. There was one eyewitness
who claimed to have been in the house when this crime
occurred, and there was an audio tape with the voice of
someone claiming to have committed the crime. But as
far as Frank was concerned, that voice could've belonged
to anyone. Hell, it could've been the prosecutor! He
didn't put anything past them. He'd seen prosecutors in
cases fabricate evidence just to obtain a conviction, and
knowing Roger Dean's history, anything was possible.

Frank Wolfman had a reputation for being a champion
for drug kingpins and criminals, with blood money to
spend on his extremely high retainer fee. He was the
mouthpiece gangsters sought around the country. And
if he had it his way, Lil' Bert would walk out of the
courtroom a free man. He really didn't care if his new
client was guilty. He was hired to ensure that Roger Dean
didn't back down on his deal. If he did, Frank Wolfman

and his team were ready to retry this case in the court of public opinion, especially when he was aware of Roger Dean's porn tape.

A crowd of police officers stormed into the courtroom for moral support as they had done at Lil' Bert's first trial. The facts in the case weren't about to change, just turn ass backward with details acquired to make the district attorney's office look incapable of protecting the citizens of Philadelphia.

Judge Sebo, his face looking a little congested, sat down and set the hearing in motion.

District Attorney Roger Dean went straight to the point, presenting his motion to withdraw all charges against Alberto 'Lil' Bert' Ruiz. "Your Honor, in the interest of justice, the district attorney's office of the City of Philadelphia presented to this court a motion to withdraw all charges against the defendant. In light of new evidence available to us, we believe there is no legal reason beyond a reasonable doubt that the defendant's conviction could stand in any civilized society." Roger Dean's nostrils distended slightly as he took his seat at the prosecutor's table.

There was a suspended moment in the courtroom, then an outburst. The cops in attendance were yelling and screaming.

"This is bullshit!"

"He's a cop killer!"

"Quiet in the courtroom! Quiet in the courtroom!" The judge was banging his gavel. The commotion went on for several more seconds before order was finally restored. The chaos in the courtroom came to a standstill.

Frank Wolfman was unruffled but amazed by the theatrics of Roger Dean's performance. Judge Sebo's face was redder than a stop sign. The spectators in the courtroom were angry but confidant, because Judge Sebo was a law-and-order judge. But he fooled the packed courtroom when he ordered a direct acquittal.

Everyone in the courtroom remained seated, enjoying the way Judge Sebo was chewing Roger Dean out for wasting taxpayers' money on a trial when his office was not sure if they had the right person. The whole hearing took half an hour, and Lil' Bert walked out of the Criminal Justice Center a free man with a mission in mind and feeling invincible.

Immediately after the court hearing, Roger Dean met Shareef at Pat's Cheesesteaks in South Philly, and he picked up his porn tape. "Here it is, Mr. DA." Shareef handed Roger Dean the DVD wrapped in a paper bag.

"If I find out there's another copy, I will come after you with the full weight of the law." Dean grabbed the DVD and snapped it in half.

"I know you will. You will never see me again." Shareef walked away, and he looked over his shoulder. "Unless of course you get caught with your dick out again."

Seventy-two hours later, Lil' Bert was forced to fulfill the promise he made to his grandmother, Maria, to visit his father's grave. As he knelt in front of Detective Ruiz's tombstone faking a prayer, Maria hovered over him with her .25-caliber in hand. When Bert tilted his head up, he felt the blast crushing against his skull. His body slumped on top of Detective Ruiz's grave.

Amazingly, Lil' Bert was not dead as he lay facedown with his eyes glued against Detective Ruiz's photo attached to his tombstone.

"Justice comes in different ways, son. As much as I came to love you, I loved your father more!" Maria felt the heavy load she had been carrying since her son's death lifted.

Lil' Bert wanted to plead for his life, but he was unable to speak. He was now in the position he had put so many others. He was now sorry for all the murders he committed. It was the first time he could empathize with anyone, but it was too late. He was about to pay the consequence of a life lived dirty.

Maria looked down at Lil' Bert, blew him a kiss, and squeezed the trigger two more times.

"Now you can meet your father, you son of a bitch!" She looked down at Lil' Bert and watched the blood pour out of the gaping wounds in his body. She had avenged her son's death, and she felt closure. She was remorseful that it was at the expense of her grandson, but when you live a life of crime and murder like Bert did, it's only a matter of time before your number is up.

The next morning, the cemetery caretakers found the body of an unidentified man slumped on top of a grave. The corpse was later identified as Alberto "Lil' Bert" Ruiz, a suspected cop killer. Forensic pathologists in Philadelphia removed three .25-caliber slugs from Bert's brain, tested them, and discovered that the bullets were laced with garlic.

As always, an investigation was launched, and the streets of Philly were crying foul play on behalf of the police. The investigation of Lil' Bert's death was dead in its infancy. The public interest in the case languished, and the DA's office was more than happy to classify the case as unsolved.

Epilogue

A year after Lil' Bert's death, District Attorney Roger Dean ran for Commonwealth judge, winning the seat that was left open by Judge Tommy Sebo, who died of a heart attack.

Maria Vasquez Ruiz, Lil' Bert's grandmother, still lives in Philadelphia with no regrets. After her act of revenge on Lil' Bert, she became the founder of her own organization in Philadelphia called Mothers of Murder Victims, which provides scholarships to children of police officers who have been killed in the line of duty.

Tete still lives in a rehabilitation center in North Philadelphia. She's been trying to walk again. When she jumped out the window when Black Manny shot it out with cops, she broke her spine and is a quadriplegic. She still gets her groove on right from her wheelchair, giving the best neck pussy a nigga could ask for.

Fat Angel, aka Willie Gomez, aka Twenty, was arrested again and sentenced to life without parole in the Feds. Despite being a rat for the government in over fifty cases, he couldn't escape the murder charge he caught down in Brick City. Unfortunately, he was stabbed to death in his cell at the U.S. Penitentiary in Atlanta.

Three Finger June disappeared right after Lil' Bert was found guilty. Rumors on the block are that someone down in Puerto Rico slit his throat and left him to die.

In a twist of fate, Shyla and Jackie Delsmith met each other when Shyla went to the Western Union office to apply for a job as a correctional officer. They have been licking and twisting each other's kittens ever since. Shyla is now a correctional officer at Graterford Prison.

After being released from prison, Ali Jones hooked up with Jackie Delsmith and Shyla. He lives with them out in South Philly. Like the true grimy nigga he is, he got both of them pregnant with his children.

Nice-town Shareef is still the North-side Don, supplying every up-and-coming drug dealer in Philly with whatever they need. His number one product is H, and Maria Vasquez is his main connection.

MaryLuz's and her son Ito's deaths are still unsolved. Atlanta police have a $50,000 reward out, but they haven't been able to come up with any leads.

Author's Note

This book was originally titled *Cop Killer: Murder in the Badlands,* but due to the recent violent sprees that claimed the life of six police officers in Philadelphia, the title was changed to avoid any controversy with the law enforcement community.

Nevertheless, the content remains the same.

"Importance of Fatherhood"

by Lee Anthony "Blame" Fox

Lawless Intent is more than a book of fiction.
It's a depiction of the importance of fatherhood.
Not a broke down in the way nigga that's no good,
Who just wants to plant seeds in chicks in the
'hood,
And rolls, ignores the mother of his seeds,
And calls them bitches and hoes.
Oh No!
That shit ain't right, but it's happening.
Niggas need to get smacked and put on track,
Stop the bullshitting rap and get with the facts.
Nigga, you're a father!
Man up!
And if you're not ready,
Then why bother to call yourself a man?
Nigga, you gotta understand,
That your lil' man is pussy's biggest fan,
And the pussy's like quicksand,
Sucking in your lil' man's clan.
So be ready for the planned and unplanned,
'Cuz a child needs a father in his or her life to teach
'em,
What's wrong and what's right,
And hold 'em tight and tuck 'em in at night,

And basically be that guiding light.

A child needs his or her father to lead, help 'em succeed,

And prepare 'em 4 when they have their own seeds.

A child needs a father,

Not a coward who won't bother to be a father to his seeds,

Take care of his responsibilities and be a real man.

Damn!

I just don't understand.

Why not appreciate,

And accept your gift from the Creator of man?

Something so sweet and filled with love

You fucking scrubs.

A man you isn't, and not ever was,

'Cuz your seeds are fatherless and in need of your love.

The importance of fatherhood is for chicks too.

You know, the ones who like being bitches and hoes

With mad dicks to run thru.

The ones who play games 'cuz a nigga don't want you.

So, you use the child as a tool,

To make 'em feel pain as you do.

That shit ain't cool.

If a nigga wants to be there,

Let 'em be there.

The child shouldn't suffer 'cuz y'all relationship ain't going nowhere.

It's not fair for the child to be raised by one parent,

While he or she has two there.

The importance of fatherhood is real.

As for them chicks that run thru dicks,

Turning tricks, not giving a shit,
Now that's some bullshit!
Seriously, it's sad.
You mad 'cuz you don't know who you gave the
pussy to
And who's your baby's dad.
You're left crying, child fatherless.
Everyone else laughs, ma,
Protect that ass!
Only let real men smash,
'Cuz in the end, it'll be them that'll last.
Fatherhood,
The importance of it goes a long way.
Guidance is needed, so they won't be led astray,
Lost in the street-life or blown away,
Boxed-up or locked-up, not seeing the light of day.
The importance of fatherhood is needed
And is not ever going away.
A real man, a father, a pop, a dad
It's something the (Cop Killa) really never had.

"Where Have All the Fathers Gone"

by Amanda Buchanan Winkey

Why are they trading in natural habits blessed by God, for unnatural ones?

Because it's natural to love your child no matter what.

It's unnatural to leave your child in the name of lust.

A man condemns himself by his words.

He lies to his children and his wife, just so he can sneak out late at night.

While his son is doing time who left a girlfriend and son behind.

Men have become lovers of themselves while cascading gently through hell. With their minds set on money, wealth, and fame, leaving in their wake nothing but heartaches and pain.

Never once, thinking about the children who have made hell their home, in search of a father who promised their mother, that he would never leave them alone.

The wrath of God is upon you all. Because, fathers are needed both big and small, to be comforter for these children in a world that is lost. Father why pay the cost, when all you have to do is help a little girl or a little boy?

Glossary

ahora: now
ven aqui: come here
bodega: store
beef: problems
birds: kilos of cocaine
cabron: a motherfucker
cuchifrito: name of a type of Spanish restaurant
cats: guys
crack-a-lacking: what's happening
crack whore: a person who has sex for crack
comprende: understand
culo: ass
cura: cure
dat: that
dawg: friend
fa sure: for sure
familia para siempre: family forever
hara: police
hijoito: little son
hood rat: a girl who sleeps with anyone in the hood
jake: police
la cura: the cure
manteca: heroin
mamao: sucker
maricon: motherfucker
mira mi: look at me
mi hijo: my son

MS-13: a national Hispanic gang
nada: nothing
negro susio: dirty black motherfucker
po-po: the police
porque: why?
pendejo: a sucker
perdon: I'm sorry
que pasar?: what's happening?
quien es?: who is it?
Satana: Satan
si, Papi: yes, Daddy